COFFEE

with

GHOSTS

CRAIG DRAHEIM

Coffee With Ghosts
Copyright © 2024 by Craig Draheim

ISBN: 979-8894790152(sc)
ISBN: 979-8894790169(e)

All rights reserved. No part of this publication may be reproduced, distributed, or transmitted in any form or by any means, including photocopying, recording, or other electronic or mechanical methods, without the prior written permission of the publisher and/or the author, except in the case of brief quotations embodied in critical reviews and other noncommercial uses permitted by copyright law.

The views expressed in this book are solely those of the author and do not necessarily reflect the views of the publisher, and the publisher hereby disclaims any responsibility for them.

The Reading Glass Books
(888) 420-3050
www.readingglassbooks.com
fulfillment@readingglassbooks.com

"…Dear Sir or Madam will you read my book it took me years to write, will you take a look…"

Beatles—<u>Paperback Writer</u>

Contents

PROLOGUE

According to the dictionary, the prologue is supposed to be the introduction, and a foreword is one as well, although intended to be written by someone other than the author. A foreword would be nice, but that's for the popular, known, established, blah, blah, blah. Being none of the aforementioned, I will probably be even less if this book is ever published. However, if you're anything like me, as a reader, you'd skip the introduction and go directly to the first chapter, diving into the story without the influence of the disclaimer. Many times, the prologue is nothing more than a generalized pontification, a vent for the author to further sway the reader into the same mindset. So, it can feel too hot or too cold, like sticking your toes barely into the surface of a lake, which is seldom an indication of the temperature below or how you'll feel once submerged into its depths.

I always thought the hardest part of getting a book published was writing it. Man, was I a fool! Writing the book is the easy part. Trying to get published stinks. You must wade through a lot of shit to have your story put on the shelves of a bookstore. It also takes a great deal of endurance, a whole lot of luck, and a charismatic personality, or at least good looks. Okay, maybe looks have nothing to do with it, but you need some advantage, rabbits' foot, uncle in the business, something. So really, the chance of this story being run by the press is slim at best. After all, for this manuscript to go anywhere, it'll have to pass through the hands of the very people that I slander.

Like any trying-to-get-published freshman, I got the starter books. There are writers' market catalogs that are supposed to tell you what literary agents would want to represent you or what publishing houses would be frothing at the mouth to get ahold of your manuscript. Or at least that's what the editors and assistant editors who now write these books want you to believe. And like a complete moron, I bought everyone, reeled in by a quote on the front cover by a famous selling author calling the catalog one of the most valuable tools for a "writer new to the marketplace." The humor in this is that the famous author probably hasn't had to bother with the mood swings of an agent or editor since Bret Easton Ellis was in diapers (I can't believe I just said "in diapers").

How would he know how helpful it is? Oh, it can be helpful, but certainly not to the new and unpublished author. That is a new and unpublished author who has no celebrity status, a wealthy spouse, or a close friend at a publishing house who shares the same interior decorator. This is 2003 and publishing is becoming a blood sport, spilling ink from the veins of all those starry-eyed dramatists, essayists, and poets, onto some obscure pages, never to be read by anyone other than close family and friends, because the price for marketing is far too much for it to ever really be exposed to the world.

I surfed the internet for advice and received so much information that it all canceled itself out: get an agent, don't get an agent, go directly to the publishing house, don't go, self-publish, don't think it's vain, etcetera. I subscribed to writers' magazines for all the latest tips and sent query letter upon query letter, some creatively poignant and others boringly concise for the jaded. I joined a couple writers' groups where we all sat around and tried to be fair to each other while eating stale pastries, but that turned out to be a bunch of crap as well. No one was ever really impressed with another person's writing, and if they were, jealousy always made the critique a little harsher. And if someone was impartial, they'd come up with an overly extended critique just to sound sophisticated.

Is that all a self-esteem issue? Probably, but I don't know that self-esteem plays an important role for writers. If anything, being neurotic and tripping over your own insecurities would be an asset. Maybe I should make myself a little clearer. What I'm mostly referring to are writers of fiction, not non-fiction. Non-fiction writers need a great deal of self-confidence. After all, they should be somewhat of an authority in whatever they're putting to print. We fiction writers like to tell the truth as well, we only like to do it anonymously. We'll weave a grudge in a mystery thriller, make up for our short comings in an action adventure, or give notice to our boring lives by writing a "literary novel," where we simply change the names and places of actual events to insure that the protagonist, who is really one of us in fiction drag, is able to make the political statements and personal accusations that our friends have found trite many months and even years before. But I'm digressing (cliché).

I went to seminars and workshops given by regionally popular authors. And I went to hear speeches given by nationally known authors. I bought copies of their books and had them sign inside the covers. When I asked them how they became published, they all had anecdotes instead of answers. Either they just wanted to get me out of the way for the cute college student standing behind me or they didn't want to give away the secret handshake to their club. So, when I signed up for a seven-day conference in Louisville and had the opportunity to live and circulate with people who had cracked the publishing code, plus spend a great deal of time in the company of other struggling writers like me, minus the stale pastries, I was certain something good would come out of it. It was hard to contain my excitement. I was overwhelmed by daydreams that had me walking away with a book deal, knowing at the end of the conference that an agent and/or editor would be waiting for my novel. I had scenes that I played repeatedly in my mind where I came back home and told my boss to go fuck himself. Not in his office but in front of coworkers, where they could marvel at my rebellion. I saw myself telling my wife pretty much the same thing and then taking my daughter for a month-long vacation to Disney World on the advancement they'd pay me. Plus, I had other reasons why I needed my story to be published.

Like many of my comrades, especially those in Louisville, I started writing late in life, though I had the bug at a much younger age. I always thought there was plenty of time, reassuring myself with examples like James Thurber, who started later in life. But maybe that was a tall tale. A teacher told me that once, and I never thought to research the life of Mr. Thurber. For all I know, he could've been writing short stories when he had pimples and his voice was changing.

I almost want to say I started out too late, but I don't want to discourage other writers or people like me wanting to get out of that ho-hum, degrading, and unthankful job, because there certainly are those miracle success stories, how few they may be. But it's a much more embarrassing and compromising life than you think. If you thought it was bad working on an assembly line in some small factory where your coworker who calls you dude, is half your age, makes a dollar more an hour than you, and is in charge of making sure you wrap, stamp, ground, press, sand, or mark something the right way, it pales in comparison to how condescending, patronizing, or humiliatingly rude people in the literary business can be.

I believe that if you have the desire to write, write. If nothing else, it's good therapy. Although I'm certain that there are a lot of Virginia Woolf's and Robert Frosts out there who never put pen to hand. Then again, there are those Virginia Woolf's and Robert Frosts who did put pen to hand and their work, no matter how fresh, may never be brought to light. Instead, I just want hopeful writers to be prepared and thick-skinned. Literature is a big business, and I don't mean there are a lot of readers out there waiting for your book to come out in paperback. I mean that there are a lot of people waiting to make money off those of us with an active imagination, and that's not so much for our material, as for our desire to bring it into the light.

The most I can gain from one of my stories making it to market is that my daughter will always know that I'll be there for her. The least is an obligation to share with other writers or those that are considering it as a possible career change. Rejections are powerful, even the subtle ones. And the more personally attached you are to your manuscript, the more devastating the rejections seem. Though this is redundant and a no brainer to those who've been through the mill. However, a writer always writes, no matter their motivation or situation. Sometimes it consumes us because it becomes a big part of our life– an undisclosed memoir. But it's not the only part of our lives. It is a need for most writers because it not only helps us to discover who we are, but many times where we need to be.

By Saturday, I was still pissed and confused, wondering why I was here. I felt like the whole business of writing stunk. The week seemed to have turned into a farce, really, to bargain with people who had exclusive claims on marketing the written word, with six literary agents sitting on the panel. No, actually, they ended up sitting in a row behind two long tables pushed together in a 50' x 50' room with only a 9-foot-high ceiling, and thinking they deserved better, they stuck to sitting at eye level and were unable to peer down on their audience of fifty writers. Oh, I take that back, forty-nine writers. God, they knew all the questions us poor wannabe writers were going to ask. I could read it in them, and it sickened me. It sickened me because it's become such a routine for them. But they were good. All six of them, trust me, acting as though every question is original, sitting with bated breath and replying with that well-rehearsed look of concern. However, a condescending note trailed their voices, and all but a few of the writers could pick out the cord, and some even sensed what I read; that not one of them at that time had any intention of taking on any new clients.

These shits are trained apes—all of them. No, I take that back. They're trained beavers, building dams against a struggling class writer. Preventing us from allowing our creative juices to flow. Boy did that sound sappy. Anyway, these agents would've complained about the conditions if they didn't like the free trip, business write-off, and adoration. It's true, they didn't show it on the surface, but they liked the control and power, playing grownup in front of their nervous and less savvy peers. They were the thirteen-year-old girl babysitting her eight-year-old brother. All smug and well-educated pricks with sheep skins from Ivy League colleges knowing not to display any superiority in their interviews. But their colors still rained through the evening before dinner. They were used to being difficult in New York restaurants. Some of the attendees were able to watch them, and it was disarming for those who really thought they had a chance and then wondering if they'd look as embarrassed as the waitresses did.

These were the goddamn professionals. The cream of the crop. They had a reputation for living up to it. The New York experience for writers. Please,

I've never seen so many narrow-minded liberals in all my life. But these assholes knew that they were needed, wanted, and even desired, and that's a good feeling for them. Well, hell, for anyone right? Maybe their bodies weren't desired— except, of course, for the blonde agent that was sitting in the middle with the vee-cut black top and the brunette on the end if she would've loosened up a little bit and get that bug out of her ass. Then again, her attitude did excite a couple of the guys. But they were desired because they held the chance for everyone at the conference to make a name for themselves, and that's what everyone wanted to do.

Few at the conference liked their lives or the way they were treated. They all wanted to be treated better. Who could blame them? I mean who can blame anyone for wanting to be treated better? Honestly? Being a writer seemed like a way to be treated better. Consider all the ads that tell us to follow our dreams. This was it for a lot of them–not exactly spring chickens. Most thought of this new career path as the end of the road, knowing they weren't going to get very far in the jobs or lifestyles they currently had. They wanted to travel in the circles and society that those jaded professionals did. They wanted to live, be recognized, and not feel like another unheard apparition. They wanted to be given the same respect. Or at least have someone once kiss their ass. But it didn't look like that was going to happen to anyone Saturday morning. Well, not for unpublished writers anyway. Nonetheless, most everyone thought there was one last chance, even me. Can you imagine? I could see through these people, proving that conferences were becoming increasingly less an opportunity for new authors and more of an opportunity for literary agents to get away, as well as published authors to milk their own self-worth. And yet there I was another bonehead thinking my manuscript was going to be picked up as the breakaway novel for the year. No matter what, you seem to always hang onto that fleeting chance. But this is too far ahead in the story. Let me back up a little bit.

The first day of this story really began six days prior, on Sunday with writers arriving from morning till night. For most it wasn't the first time, they've been coming to this conference every year. For a few though, it was the first time, coming with high expectations, and thinking their writing was the best. Little did they know it wasn't. It wasn't because they didn't think anyone else could really write. They knew no one else at home could because no one at home really understood their material, their artistic vision.

Everyone smiled when they walked into the dorm where they were supposed to check in. Many were familiar with one another, shared a hug or a handshake, and then got their room key from Jim Laird, this year's new director. Some lingered around wanting to see who was coming in. Some went straight to their rooms to unpack and set up shop for the week, even putting a family picture on their desks. A few went immediately to lunch or dinner. That's what Jim wanted to do, asking two of the participants he knew from previous conferences if they would pick him up a burger from McDonald's. He had to stick around to check everyone in as they showed up. The two people that went to McDonald's took a very long time, and it seemed to him that neither of them were giving him their undivided attention when he requested the number one combo without lettuce.

Grace arrived at two. This was her third year with the Red Creek Writers Conference. She can be described as a slut, though that's not accurate. She's beautiful, and everyone wants to have sex with her, and she likes having sex, but then who doesn't on their own terms? She knew men wanted her ever since she could remember. She even turned a lot of women on with the way she swaggered, including borderline lesbians who secretly admired her openness. In an orgy she would be the center, the focus, the one everyone else wanted to touch. Her confidence never faltered, ever since she knew that she was desirable. The only problem with that is that she sometimes appeared like a starlet in a B movie with exaggerated laughter while leaning forward and holding back her head while showing off straight white teeth, then finishing off with the toss of her hair. Jim couldn't think of her as desirable, though. He couldn't see her climbing into bed with him. If she did, he'd have to start writing comedy instead of drama, feeling the affair would be too unfathomable to be taken seriously. Besides, everyone knew the big reason she was here. She wanted to fuck Joey Goode. He's one of the published authors that attended to give classes on how to get published, find your voice, that sort of shit.

Jim knew if he asked Grace, she'd go get him something to eat. Because of her looks, most people wouldn't impose. However, Jim knew where he stood with her. Besides, he wanted a burger, and the longer he had to wait the more time he had to think about what he really wanted.

"Hey Grace, why don't you get me one of those olive burgers at Rascolli's?"

"What do I look like, your slave? Why don't you ask Oscar?"

Oscar was in the lobby, sitting on one of the cushioned chairs. He was the only black person at the conference, attending for five years in a row.

Oscar put down the paper and looked above his reading glasses. Oscar is forty- five and has been working on the same horror novel since before he had to wear glasses. He got the story and structure right the first time, but because he became too impatient with rejections by agents and editors that barely read his query letters, he began changing the ending, plot, what or who was doing the killing, introducing new characters, and so on. All because he thought he had to do something to make it more marketable. Patience would have been more marketable for him. The story started out simply, with hunters in northern Minnesota coming up missing. Then bodies turned up in the thaw of the spring under the snow, their death undetermined other than natural causes, but both young and old men seemed to fall victim. It was only during the winter that they were killed, year and year again. And oddly, the bodies remained fresh, as if they were just murdered, but as soon as they were found decomposition began. Oscar worried that before long he would see his premise as one of the *X Files* episodes.

Oscar looked over at Jim, still over the edge of his glasses. "Come on, Grace," Jim persisted.

"Oh, alright. You gonna buy mine too?"

"Sure."

"Oscar, you want something?" Grace asked Jim to grab a ten while she walked towards him.

"No thanks, dear."

The Welty campus is part of Faulkner University but separate and located on the east side of Louisville.

Whereas the main part of the university is located near central Louisville. Though a prime piece of real estate and comfortably low-key, the buildings on the Welty campus are less desirable, boxy, cracking red brick, with connecting awnings. Noah Petermann, nicknamed War Correspondent (though never told to his face) for his self-published book about his experiences up to and during World War two, often describes settings of where he's at, to get in the mood for writing. Two conferences ago he described the buildings and grounds as follows:

"A costly mistake, uninspiring, cracking, peeling, echoing tombs for creativity, randomly placed on a nice plush lawn like items for a yard sale. Military barracks have more character and a more liberal sense. Obviously, these structures were built at a time when contractors hired by the city were under little scrutiny or the building inspectors had a lot to gain by saying very little. It's a cross between industry and academia where industry has refused to yield. The furniture, built by prisoners and bought at retail in quantity, gives the living quarters a comfort level of being in a mental ward."

Still, War Correspondent has come here every year to spend his time in the trenches. He rarely participated in evening drinks, but he liked this group of people, though it didn't show, and he would never tell anyone. After all, almost everyone was younger than he was and less experienced, but experience sometimes takes ink from the pen and makes a person less ingenious. His writing was stodgy. He admired Hemingway and tried to impersonate his style because he felt they were kindred spirits, but in the last year he felt he was losing the ability to write. Not just a writer's block, but to herd words, give simple detail, and give directions. He hoped this conference would jar something lose, give his retirement more purpose.

At 7:30 PM, all but one of the writers had shown up for the conference. Everyone was mingling, talking, laughing, glancing at everyone else in the room, and taking their own personal inventory. Jim wanted to get the introduction over with. Bobbie approached him. She was the founder of the organization and has directed every conference since, except for this year.

"If everybody's here, Jim, I don't see why we can't get the show started." She spoke with a soft southern twang that seemed impervious to accents.

"Well, one of the new guys hasn't shown up yet."

"Which one's that?"

"The guy from Sturgeon Bay, Wisconsin. He's with Joey's group."

"Did this guy pay his deposit yet?"

"Oh, he paid everything in full. And when I talked to him on the phone, he was very excited about coming. Apparently, this is the first conference he's ever been to."

"Well, I guess we'll stick it out until 8 o'clock, and if he's not here by then, we'll start without him."

"Sure." Jim had just started developing hemorrhoids before he left Cleveland, but standing and pacing in the same area all day long was taking its toll on his feet as well. He was flat-footed and had new shoes that he bought for the conference. The hemorrhoids were also drying and becoming itchy, making him feel as though he had to wipe his ass and that he was going to have shit stains in his underwear. Jim wanted to recline for the last five hours, lay back and put his hands behind his head, or lay on his side in a fetal position. He watched Grace intently because she was the one to watch. By keeping his eyes on her, he'd eventually be able to check out everyone in the room. She made her rounds, hanging her arms around old members and then introducing herself to the new ones. She loved attention for many reasons—good or bad, it didn't matter, just so long as she was remembered. But unlike other writers, she sincerely liked being with people. This also made her a poor writer. Despite having good ideas, the feeling of loneliness wouldn't allow her to get much work done before she had to make contact with the outside world. It also kept her from having a steady boyfriend or husband, as she got bored quickly and always wanted a change.

Grace went to conferences, because above all other people, she liked the environment of writers. She could say almost anything to them. She could be shocking and get away with it, hoping at times it would provide fodder for one of their stories. It never did though. The people that got to know her either thought that she was anything but a noteworthy character and too stereotypical, even too outgoing. If they needed a model for uninhibited beauty, using her they felt they'd have to suffer the brunt of her forwardness, but she would've relished it. Writers largely have open minds, except when it comes to editors, but their demeanor is almost always conservative. Grace knew this, so she enjoyed trying to make their actions match their writing. That's mostly why she liked sex with Joey Goode. He had a clean-cut appearance, direct with his words and speech, white and successful. Plus, he was married. She wanted him to take care of her, but she wanted more to watch him lick her pussy. She had a fetish for watching him lose all his social decency for those minutes, when he was on top, she made him talk to her and say how hard he was going to fuck her, but the words were always less creative than his writing. Although her beauty was encouraging, trying to think up something new to please her sometimes stalled the moment. When she'd catch this, she would put her hand over his mouth so he could concentrate and ejaculate. And when he came it was the highlight of their time together. His body jolted in little spasms, and he would hold his mouth open while curling his lips. Showing his teeth made him look animal and primitive for the moment. This is what Grace wanted to achieve. It was better in the darkness with a faint light to show his outline. Grace thought of it as his transforming into a beast, a werewolf, and this made her high knowing she had that sort of affect.

Grace wrote erotica slash romance, and if she could write exactly what she said to others, she would've been good at it. If only she could avoid living it, she would have the literary success she admired in Joey. But the interactions between her characters went as follows:

"Derek wanted to taste every inch of Amanda, those luscious, rounded knolls, unblemished buttock, and grass covered abyss. The saliva excreted profusely in his mouth and the semen activity in his genitals accelerated to the speed of light. His steel shaft being tempered and hardened from Amanda's heat. Amanda didn't want his kisses. She wanted his penetration, first in her pleading mouth and then between her praying thighs. She wanted that firm, well-oiled hydraulic machine to pump in and out of her, to strike oil."

This is where Joey's background as a stage actor was essential, especially if he wanted to get laid. He couldn't take her writing seriously. It was crap. But because he didn't have her in one of his groups yet, he could tell her "It needs a little work, but you definitely have found your voice." This is what made Joey feel dirty, not the cheating on his wife, but the fact he was telling her things that he wouldn't tell college students where he taught in Alabama, if just to help encourage them. She was a hack, but she was dynamic and gorgeous. She had a voice, but she rarely showed it on paper. She'd rather talk about it.

The guy from Wisconsin never showed up. Jim was going to call in the morning if he hadn't arrived by then. At eight o'clock, Jim asked for everyone's attention, passed around a schedule for the week, and introduced all the published authors who were group leaders and would be giving the classes. Everyone paired off with their groups and went into vacant rooms so they could discuss what to expect. The new attendees couldn't believe how casually the published authors sat and talked with them. One author was a first-time participant. Tom Finnigan was better known in the western states, having written pop culture mysteries and dramatic plays of an individual's internal struggle. He was also a musician and owned a small multimedia company that put together modest theater productions, short films, and jazz concerts. Though Irish, he had a

Greek and Italian look about him and dressed very west coast, seldom without his shades.

Tom's group consisted of two housewives from the suburbs of Chicago whose kids were in their teens and twenties, one twenty-six-year-old lady that worked at a Barnes & Noble book store, a female clinical therapist that just celebrated her thirty first birthday two days prior, telling her friends after two margaritas how old she was getting and hasn't accomplished anything in her life. And finally, there was a sixty three year old grandmother that runs a writers group out of her church basement on week nights. This was for anyone out of her town of five hundred in Tennessee that cares to attend and wants to bring a dish to pass. All in the group had a full manuscript, though unpolished.

"Hello everyone. I thought we'd just get to know each other a little bit, what we hope to get from this conference, a little about our past…You know that sort of thing." They were one of the lucky groups, being able to sit out in the lobby of the dorm, whereas most others had to bunch up in one of the small rooms and sit on the single beds. Tom's group put their chairs close and around in a circle as if preparing for an intervention. The Chicago wives, Liz, and Beverly, sat on either side of Tom. Neither of them had aspirations for an affair with him. After all he was "so cosmopolitan," but they were going to show him how witty they could be. What they wanted was his agent, or to be referred to another agent by him, or at the least to be recommended to a publishing house. Both had completed manuscripts of unsolved murder and mayhem. Liz's novel was about a young serial killer that travels across the United States during the late sixties, killing drifting vagabonds and hitchhiking hippies. The story was written like a memoir by the killer now in the present day and never caught. Beverly's was about a small-town barber in Indiana that gets blamed for his sister's murder after love letters are found by investigators in her house showing an illicit affair between the two. The taboo relationship alone discourages anyone to look any further, until a street smart, wise cracking private detective who was traveling cross country on a vacation stumble haphazardly into the case. Like the characters in their stories, both Liz and Beverly tried avoiding the truth with Tom. They wanted to turn the conversation quickly to their stories. Neither wanted to explain their days of cleaning house, trips to Disney World, their son being on the basketball team, or their daughter going on her first date. "We'll have plenty of time this week to talk and discuss our manuscripts.

Right now, I'd just like to hear about yourself. What got you into writing. You know." Liz liked it that Tom put his hand on her knee when he said that, but she thought he treated her a bit childish. The twenty-six-year-old book store clerk was rocking on the two back legs of the chair she pulled away from the table. She lost her balance and fell backward.

"Are you alright?" Tom got up from his chair to help, but the young lady was already up.

"Yeah, I'm fine." She kept her head down picking her chair back up. She was embarrassed and obviously unhurt. Liz restarted the discussion.

"Well, when you said, 'what we hope to get from the conference', I figured that meant to talk about our books. Beverly and I would like to know how to get published, but we both know that our material may need polishing before an agent sees it." Liz almost said that with a challenge in her voice, and it was one of the few times Beverly wished Liz hadn't included her. What Liz really wanted to say was, "Look, I'm a mother of two teenage boys and a daughter in college. I came to this conference to get something published so I can finally have a life of my own. I paid to attend this thing, and I don't give a shit if you're Norman Mailer. I'm going to get something else out of it other than couch talk."

"We'll get to that stuff. We've got all week and a lot of classes that will cover the industry." Tom made quotation gestures when he said industry. "I just thought this would be a good time to break the ice and get to know each other, considering we'll be having quite a few group meetings as well."

All the other groups were doing much the same thing, getting acquainted. Because of the drive or the flight, none of the published authors had the energy to start any technical discussions about writing or marketing. Other than a desperate few, most of the wannabees didn't want to jump into that either. They wanted to size up the people they were going to tell the intimate details of their stories to. A large amount of the manuscripts at the conference had sex scenes, brutal killings, or details of loneliness or regret that were inspired by personal hardship. To read any of that aloud, they wanted to ensure that these were people unlike the ones at home. Joey and Denise Domikowski, another published writer, spent less time with their groups and more time talking to each other, both having a background in acting. This made Grace jealous, and being that she was assigned to Denise's group, it gave her an excuse to call her away and ask questions concerning the week's events. Joey got the message and returned to his group.

Jim was pried from a deep sleep and a twisted dream by the ring of his cell phone at 2:10 in the morning. He almost didn't wake up, as ringing became a part of the dream. He was talking with his ex-wife at a picnic table in a park somewhere. It was bright and sunny. Couples were on the lawn around them, scattered sparsely, and all were having sex. He and his ex-wife were sitting on the same side of the table. He felt as if he almost had her talked into letting him fuck her, but in a language that made no sense, with garbled, snapping, and popping sounds. When it seemed as though she was going to agree, her cell phone rang. She got up from the table to talk, as if it were a private call and she didn't want Jim to hear. But when she did, only the top portion of her body was left, floating in midair. Her hips and legs remained seated next to Jim. For some reason it turned him on, and he couldn't help but ask her,

"Can I have this?" When she threw her phone toward him in anger, he woke up.

Jim gave all the attendees his number as an alternate, should they forget or lose the dorm number. He normally would leave it off at night, because he didn't want to pay any unnecessary roaming fees, but as he told Bobbie earlier in the evening, "I'll leave it on until we get the status on the guy from Wisconsin."

"Ahh hello."

"Jim?"

"Yeah."

"It's Barnell, Barnell Keys." Jim had to think for a couple seconds, still disoriented from sleep, then realized that Barnell was one of the new attendees.

"Yeah, Barnell, what's up?"

"I need a really big favor."

Jim had been to quite a few conferences and retreats, not including the one in Louisville. He saw several instances where writers got into trouble, but if they weren't published writers, then they were usually veteran attendees. As he drove downtown to the precinct, he couldn't remember one time when a new attendee had to be bailed out of jail. If Jim wasn't so tired that evening, he wouldn't have minded helping, but the last few days have been a pain in the ass, with tying up loose ends at work, the drive down to the conference, and then setting everything up. His reaction on the phone became rude, causing Barnell to be overly apologetic and reemphasizing to Jim that he'd be reimbursed once Barnell could get back to the room and get his check book.

After posting bail and then seeing Barnell, Jim found it impossible to be pissed off. Barnell was twenty-eight years old, but still looked as though he had just graduated from high school. There was no question that he was a geek and a nerd, an obvious part of his DNA. More still, it looked as though it was a culture that he came from, like an immigrant who crossed the Atlantic to the cool world where he blatantly stood out like an alien. He wore new Levi's that looked as though they had yet to be put through the wash and may have been baggier than he intended on his skinny legs. His light blue jacket was zipped up tight, showing only a sliver of the green checkered design in the collar of the shirt he wore underneath. His straight, light brown hair barely covered the tops of his ears, but his bangs, combed forward, covered his forehead, and at the rim of his glasses they curled to one side. The glasses looked heavy, with thick brindle frames and wide lenses.

Before he even noticed Jim on the other side of the large shuffling office, Barnell seemed intent on biting a piece of nail off one of his fingers that appeared hard to get at as he was using both hands to position the finger just right. The policeman who led him in was laying out a paper on the counter for him to sign. Only after Barnell signed it did he look up and notice Jim. He half smiled cautiously at Jim and waved. The department could've kept Barnell overnight, stalling and dragging its feet until they finally gave him any recognition. But Jim suspected they saw the same innocence he did.

Barnell stopped Jim before going outside the front doors of the station, first apologizing again and then adding, "I wasn't trying to pick up a hooker, honest. I…"

"Hey, look, Barnell. It really doesn't matter to me whether you were or not."

"Well, just for the record."

Jim chuckled a little and said, "I don't keep record, so don't sweat it."

"But really, I just pulled over to the side of the road when I saw that girl and asked for directions. I couldn't figure out how in the heck to get back to the campus."

"What were you doing in that part of town anyhow?"

"I went out for a drive to kind of look the city over. One of the ladies at the dorm gave me directions to the factory where they made the Louisville Sluggers, so I drove over there, but then I kept getting turned around on my way back. I saw that girl, and there weren't a lot of people around, so I thought it was safe."

"So, you knew she was a prostitute?" Barnell raised his shoulders with his eyebrows. Though Jim couldn't see them under his hair, he could tell from the way his eyes widened.

"Well, I had a pretty good idea by the way she was dressed."

"Why did the cops arrest you if you just asked for directions?"

"Because she was in my car."

"What? Why was she in your car?" Jim's eyebrows were raised now and easy to see, still far below his widow's peak.

"She just asked if I'd take her up the street a couple blocks so she could meet up with her friends. And I did. I didn't see any cruisers, not until it was too late."

"Too late? You mean after you dropped her off?" Though Jim worked in taxes and trusts, he was trying to think like a criminal lawyer about how Barnell's actions could be misinterpreted.

"No, when I was zipping my pants back up."

"Wha.?" Jim's mouth remained open, unable to finish the word. If his eyebrows could raise anymore, they did. He looked over his shoulder to make sure no one had snuck up and was standing next to them. "Okay, tell me you know that there's no difference between sexual relations and having sex."

"No, that's not the way it was. You've got to let me finish." Without realizing it, while Jim kept leaning in toward Barnell to try and keep their conversation private, the two of them were now in a corner by the entrance, with Barnell having his back against the wall and looking by his posture as if he were being threatened. A sergeant who had been talking with another cop since Jim first came in noticed them both as they were leaving. With the two of them still standing there and looking odd pressed up against the corner, the sergeant walked over.

"Excuse me, but if you two gentlemen don't have any business here, I'm going to have to ask you to leave." Jim and Barnell went outside and finished their conversation on the steps.

"Alright, now that you have your pants down, then what?"

"I didn't have my pants down." Barnell put his hands on his hips in frustration. He rolled his eyes and took a deep breathe. Jim noticed that he almost seemed embarrassed about the mere mention of having his pants down.

"Right after that girl got into the car and I pulled away from the curb, she lit up a joint. I thought she was lighting up a cigarette until I caught a whiff of it and looked over. I had to stop for a traffic light and was about to tell her to get rid of it, but she handed it over to me. It was just a small roach, so I took it and was going to toss it out the window. I just went through the intersection and was shifting into second when it fell out of my hand. I thought it went onto the floor, but instead it fell on my seat under my crotch. It burned a small hole in both my car seat and my pants, not to mention my testicles. I jerked the car over to the curb right when a patrol car was coming from another direction, but I couldn't stand the pain, so I had to get out of the car. The roach must have burnt up or something, because as soon as I stood up, it quit burning. By then I'm standing facing the patrol car pulled up behind my car, I have my pants unzipped and the hooker's laughing like a lunatic in the car.

I didn't want to tell the cops anything about the pot because I was afraid they'd try and get me on some kind of drug charge, so the only thing I could think of saying was that it was all a mix up, but I couldn't come up with a good excuse while my pants were undone and I had a hooker in my car. Who by the way the cops knew very well." Barnell rolled his eyes again. Jim believed him but was trying to conceive of an angle that would look better in Barnell's defense. Barnell took the silence as disbelief. "It's true, look." Barnell turned around and bent over, spreading the seat of his pants apart so Jim cold see the burnt hole. Just then, the sergeant that told them to leave the building, stepped out the door with a partner.

"You know if you guys don't leave, I'm sure there's something we can find to arrest you on."

"He was just showing me his hole."

"You're pushing your luck buddy. If you don't leave now, I'm going to take *both* of you back into the station."

3

Rain started as Jim drove back from the station with Barnell following. The weather was typical of mid-March, and it was still raining the following morning, droplets big enough to encourage umbrellas even for those that seldom use them. Two coffee pots were brewing in the lobby of the main dorm, dorm F. One was for decaf and the other for regular. Whoever made coffee had already left, leaving a note that only said, "coffee is made—both regular and decaf', but there was no indication of which was which. Jim was up and, in his jeans, and only a tee shirt from the day before. He had on house slippers that his ex-wife left him when they separated. They were pink, but they felt so comfortable that he didn't mind the comments that came along with them. He shuffled slowly over to pour himself some coffee in a Styrofoam cup. Noticing the note, he thought, "It was definitely not a non-fiction writer that wrote this."

He filled his cup half and half, that way guaranteeing some caffeine.

"Alright, that's what I'm talking about. Coffee is ready and waiting." Oscar came up behind Jim.

"Don't get too excited. One is decaf and the other is regular. Your guess is as good as mine."

"What?"

"Yeah, someone was nice enough to brew both pots but too stupid to say which is which."

"Well, we can rule out the nonfiction writers." Jim smiled. "That's what I thought."

"Morning all," Dorothy entered the room. She was a state trooper from Kansas City, Kansas. She'd been coming to this conference for three years now. She kept her hair bleached the way her husband liked it, barely reaching her shoulders, making it easier to deal with while on duty. She was solid-looking, without curves, and in her housecoat, she looked innocently middle-aged. When she had her uniform on, she looked imposing, no nonsense, even threatening.

"Morning," Oscar and Jim both returned the greeting, and both sat down at the table. Neither told Dorothy about the coffee waiting for her reaction. She poured from one of them, assuming both were regulars.

"Did everyone get a good night's sleep?"

"Oh, just lovely," Oscar replied. Dorothy looked

toward Jim as if she expected a sincere answer from him. Jim looked surprised and couldn't believe she was serious.

"What he said,"

Joan came in from outside, or rather from dorm E, walking under the connecting awning to keep out of the rain. "It's nasty out there." She didn't live far from Louisville. She was born and raised in Kentucky and is now fifty-six years old. She taught school for a short time, after she was married and after her first child. She sounded like a schoolteacher ever since, as if she was talking to a large class. Though her home was little more than a thirty-minute drive from the campus, she paid to stay in the dorm for the entire week. She told her husband that she needed time away to get some writing done. She's been coming to the conference for several years and every year she says the same thing, but the real reason is that she wants to find someone to appreciate and adore her for just a short while.

She's been married to the same man for thirty-eight years and there was nothing she has been able to do on her own but this. She was attractive when she was young, looking very proper and she is an attractive older woman, still looking very proper. She remained petite, and the gray came out in streaks making her look distinguished, and her blue eyes became sharper with age. Joan wrote essays, lots of essays. Some she entered in competitions, mostly through her church, and some she won prizes for. Now she had a compilation of essays for a book, but not one of them did she want her family to read. She wanted to find a way to get it published without her husband or two sons to know. The essays revealed too much of herself. It would crush all those that she cared for if they knew, or so she thought. She wanted other people in the world to know how she felt, not her family. She titled the collection "Domestic Prayers" with an alternate title "The Poetry of House Chores."

"Ya'all goin ta any of the classes this morning?" Joan's voice always had a ring of being upbeat because it was small like her, but she learned early how to project it and make it clear, though animated.

"I sure am." Dorothy replied with the same enthusiasm. "I want to get into Tom Finnigan's class. Isn't he sexy?" Dorothy looked toward Jim and Oscar, not expecting any sort of reaction, just realizing as she said it that there were two men in the room.

"Oh, he is simply dreamy. Don't you think, Jim?"

"Absolutely, Oscar. He is all that with a bag of chips and salsa." Jim snapped his fingers and bobbed his head at a dull, tired speed, with a disgusted smile on his face".

"Oh, come on, you two. You're not jealous, are you?" Joan smiled as she sat down at the table and peeled a banana that someone had left on top of the refrigerator.

"It depends, are you talking about Tom or that banana?"

Oscar had to put his hand over his mouth to keep from spraying his coffee. Dorothy laughed, and Jim shifted his smile to teasing, letting his eyebrows rise in pride at his accomplishment. Joan gave a chuckle that took the energy of only one breath and now feeling that everyone was watching her eat the banana, broke it off, and ate it in pieces. Jim noticed her slight embarrassment and thought for a moment how she might have something else on her mind other than her grand kids or church socials. Jim wished she did. Jim wished that she had him on her mind because Jim was always attracted to her. He tried in the past to lead their discussions toward intimacy, sitting in the lobby at night drinking rum and cokes or wine, but they were always interrupted, or the discussion turned back toward writing. Joan never felt that he was interested in her and if she ever found out he was, unfortunately she would've embarrassed him.

Grace's door flung open, adjacent to the lobby and the closest one to the center of the room. She had on white, loose cotton pajamas that draped over the curves of her body like silk. No one would notice that there was a pattern of small teddy bears in the fabric. She looked sexy even with her hair in disarray, her slouching, and no makeup.

"Do you guys know that there are people trying

to sleep?"

"Yeah, well there were people trying to sleep at 1:30 in the morning, but that didn't keep other people from banging against the wall." Jim's room was next to Grace's. There was an "Oooo" at the table. "Either you or he has awful headache today."

"What makes you think it was a *he*?" Another "Oooo." Grace walked over to the coffee pots. "Which one is which?" Oscar and Jim looked at one another.

"So, don't keep us in suspense, tell us who the lucky guy is. You never held out on us before." After asking, Dorothy leaned forward in her chair like a child waiting to hear a story.

There were three classes that morning across campus, connected to the dorms by veins of cracked and pitted concrete walks. Lenny Garring was giving a class on what he called "Faulty Characters." Essentially, it was for genre writers who introduced characters that weren't important to the plot. "Such as a person you'd meet on the street that asks the time then wants to talk about the weather," he'd say. Lenny wrote mystery novels and felt that everything should have a connection to discovery or "you'll lose the reader." Ironically, making no connection between the title and statement, his best- selling mystery to date was "Do You Have The Time," in which an innocent bystander is drawn into international intrigue after a double agent asks him the time at Saint Marks Square in Venice. Being photographed by a high-tech crime ring, they don't buy into his story, solely because he matches the description of the man they expected. There have been offers to turn it into a movie, mostly by production companies that Lenny never heard of.

Tom Finnigan was giving one of the other classes titled "Research, Get Over It." This was given to demonstrate the importance of research and to just do it and quit whining, especially for nonfiction writers. His methods were so unorthodox and experimental that if it weren't for his cool demeanor and self- confidence, everyone would've thought the class was a joke. "Alright everyone, I want you to look around the room and try and remember as much about it as you possibly can. I'll give you a few minutes." Everyone stayed seated and glanced around the room. Tom looked at various wannabes, offering a polite smile when he caught their eyes. "Okay, great, now everybody close your eyes. You're in this room, and you can see every detail, right? Now I'm going to walk around the room. And because I don't know most of your names yet, I'll touch you on the shoulder. When I do, I want you to describe the setting of this room as if you were going to put it in one of your stories."

Tom paced slowly around the room as if he had a plan, but he liked more the dramatic suspense it created. He stopped behind Barnell and settled a hand on his shoulder.

"A basement class, no windows, fluorescent

lighting suspended flush with a drop ceiling… The block walls painted white…no, plaster walls were painted white," several others, thinking they weren't being watched, peered through their squinted eyelids to double check the material of the walls, "with parallel rows of long tables and blue swivel office chairs…"

"That's good, that's good." Tom, still standing behind the young man, put his hand back on his shoulder and leaned down. "What's your name?"

"Barnell."

"Thanks, Barnell. Now for the next victim," a couple of people laughed courteously. Tom kept up the suspense and walked slowly around the room. He put his hand carefully on Joan's shoulder, but none-the-less she jerked. "Sorry to startle you."

"Oh, that's alright. I just wasn't expecting it." Joan then laughed a little, nervously.

"It's Joan, isn't it?"

"Yes, it is." She was surprised and pleased that he knew her name, considering this was his first year with Red Creek Writers.

"Okay Joan, tell me about this room." Tom kept his hand on her shoulder casually, as if he had it on top of the table. Joan thought it was nice and friendly. A gesture most men don't do today. Or at least not the ones you want to.

"The bright whiteness of the room made it cold

and clinical, as if it could either be used for surgery or teaching." There was one muffled laugh in the room. "The acoustical drop ceiling didn't absorb as much sound as it pretended to. Though unexposed, the utilities felt evident. All those pipes, the wiring, and the vent ducts were present above the panels, bringing them to life and giving them brooding and discontented life like the ticket taker at a toll booth. The dark carpet flooring appeared to be no more than tile, barely distinguishable in transition from the ceramic squares in the outside hallway." Tom glanced through the open door to make sure the floor outside the room was indeed tiled in squares. They were. "Having columns in the room for support gave it a feeling of being undependable and untrustworthy in such a small area." Tom looked at the ceiling and took his hand off Joan's shoulder. He could've listened to her further, and so could the whole class, especially with their eyes closed and her small, clear, and soothing southern voice petting them, but she was also taking away the direction that Tom wanted the class to go.

"Now those were both very good descriptions." Tom thought that was enough to have everybody open their eyes, but they didn't, some people still sat there with their eyes shut. "Okay, everyone can open their eyes now…Does anyone know what may have been lacking in those scenes?" Before anyone could raise their hands or speak out, Tom added, "And as you answer any of these questions, could you please say your name so I can learn who you are." Dorothy raised her hand. "Yes."

"My name is Dorothy, and I thought they were both very good descriptions.

It gave a feeling of the room that seemed pretty accurate."

"Okay, but that's mostly because you are in the room right now. Try and imagine never seeing the room before." There was a quiet. "Does anyone think that the size of the room might help? Or the number of tables and chairs?" Tom started counting off on his fingers, "numbers of pillars, ceiling height, number of people in the room." With that, Tom raised his eyebrows.

"Yeah, but how are we supposed to know the size of the room without measurements?" Jeff Hermann announced.

Jeff was single, never married, and spoke fast and impatiently, often at the price of his words blending. This was a personality trait he developed as a young man, right out of high school and trying to sell Kirby vacuum cleaners for his first job. Staying in sales and desperate to make money to move out of his mother's house and get away from her only enforced his change in linguistics. He won twenty thousand dollars in a state lottery several years ago, and with it, bought a topless club in the Cleveland flats. Lately, the business hasn't been doing so well. He believes the mistake was letting someone else manage it. But he got so used to having free time on his hands that he doesn't feel he could go back to a full-time job and run the business. Lately, he's been having anxiety attacks, which has made the transition seem nearly impossible.

So, at thirty-five, heavy, balding, Jeff has the first draft on a children's fantasy story about a collective body of spirits that take kids out of the present and put them into the bodies of children in the past who have never been recorded through history or recognized with some documentation to give them an existence to settle their spirit. The collective body comes in the form of one body wrapped in paper, whether littered newspapers, pages from a book nearby, paper sacks, etc. He sported a goatee, plus wearing a brown leather jacket, made him look like a night club owner of a topless bar, and a lot less the children's author.

"You could pace it off." After walking around the room while he was talking, Tom was in the back, where there was an open space of fifteen by twenty-five feet. He paced the width of the room. "Thirty feet wide by." Then he paced back toward the front of the class at the chalkboard. "Fifty feet long." He was still five feet too long. No one rebutted. "That is what research is all about, getting the details and getting the dimensions. Dimensions should be taken as a metaphor as well as a literal interpretation. Dimensions are the facts that not having, even in fiction, does not paint a clear and defining picture. You owe that consideration to the reader."

Julie Kenyara was giving the third class. She is 24, the youngest of the published and unpublished writers attending. At 23, just out of college, she had her first book on the shelves, a sci-fi set a hundred years into the future. She majored in economics at Cornell, so fiction writing wasn't a hard transition. Plus, her studies inspired her story: After eventual dominance by one world power, the global government realizes that currency has become hard to manage and a useless appendage, so this causes a collapse of paper money. Therefore, people are forced to live by bartering their trades. The more product, service, or help one performs, the more it is recorded in a "world credit bank." This is intended to give everyone an incentive to work harder for civilization. But by the end of the story, the system fails and there becomes total chaos. This all reaffirms Julie's theory that in human existence there must be obvious givers, and obvious takers, and those that fall in the middle are little more than complacent extras. Still quite young, she is gradually changing her beliefs not realizing the implications she has suggested. Though a small story and not thoroughly dissected, the controversy allowed her to reap a great deal of benefits, giving her the space and time to write her next novel, "The Revolution of The Middle People."

Being in the thick of getting her first story published with great success and the company eagerly waiting her follow up, Julie was assigned to give the class on the "Publishing Business: What Brings the Gods Down From Mount Olympus" by Red Creek Writers. She was nervous, for many reasons, the least of which being her youth, which was the greater reason that several in the room were indifferent toward her. If she were fifty and read Mien Kampf at a bar mitzvah, she would've received a warmer reception.

Warren Hess was a Vietnam War veteran from North Carolina. During the late eighties, a Japanese company bought out a small tubing factory that he was working at and offered him with retirement and benefit plans. They shipped the presses and some of the management staff elsewhere, tore down the factory, and put up a strip mall. Without a job, Warren went to work in his brother's roofing company. Not long after, he started developing knee and back problems.

He suffered it as long as he could for the sake of his brother. Now, getting hardly enough compensation for his injuries and a little more from V.A., he has returned to the writing he did as a teenager, trying to write a compelling story about the time he served "in country." Unfortunately, his story is considered to be "over done" by agents and publishers, so in the past two years he's tried to put a unique spin on it, by turning it into fiction. A couple publishers went so far as to say that they were more interested in recent wars.

His writing was good. It wasn't great, but it was plausible, better than celebrity autobiographies written with their own hand or through ghostwriters. In his new format, Warren recently broke the events down into short stories with many different protagonists and written in different narratives with plots that seemed to be truer to him now than immediately after the fall of Saigon.

Julie was an insult to Warren. He was attending her class, and she could feel him like a dog that doesn't bark but waits with a low growl, lying on its haunches until you come within the reach of its chain. In the next hour and a half, she would find out if she had to pay the price for her success, because she knew Warren. He was in her individual group as well. She read his bio and the synopsis for his stories. Everyone sent them to their instructors prior to the conference. When she tried approaching him the evening before, she felt that he was only going through the motions in his introduction and that he could care less what anyone thought of him.

Julie changed the program of her class instruction. Actually, she was ad libbing. Some of the more seasoned participants at the Red Creek conference expected that Julie would be a little nervous for her first class, but they didn't expect it to this degree. The initial impression that most would get of her is that of a young, sharp, and professional Asian woman who dresses smartly, stays fit, and has an agenda planned for every day of her life. Her short, cropped, business-cut hairstyle seemed to suggest that she has no time for a personal life and does not care for one.

Warren was a complete opposite, with jeans tattered, cowboy boots, and any shirt that suggests he neither folds nor hangs up his clothing, except maybe on a bed post. His hair was grayer than brown, long, touching his shoulders easily, never in a ponytail, and thinning on top. He's been divorced three times, has an unkept beard, and large, slow-moving eyes that made him look tired of all the bullshit, and he was. He would be considered slim if not for a beer gut.

Attendees in the class began looking around at each other with questioning and concerned brows about the credibility of the class.

"The ahhh…story may not always be…ahhh ideal for a mayor commercial publisher. Sometimes the smaller presses…"

"Excuse me," Warren held up his hand at the same time he started talking, knowing that because Julie was looking down at the floor most of the time, it would probably be a while before she saw him.

"Yes, you have a question, Mr. Hess."

"Yeah, I do, and you can call me Warren, by the way. What is a <u>mayor</u> commercial publisher?" There were a few unexpected laughs in the room. Julie looked puzzled.

"I'm sorry, I've never heard of a mayor commercial publisher."

"Well, you just said it." Julie thought for a moment, desperately, feeling the pressure of Warren's steady and unsmiling stare. Then, realizing the mistake she had made, she gave a nervous chuckle.

"Oh, I'm terribly sorry. I meant to say, "major commercial publisher." Julie looked around the room lightheartedly, but uneasily as well. She shrugged her shoulders, no one spoke, and then she continued to go on. "As I was about to say, sometimes the smaller presses or even university presses may be ideal for your work. Or. If you want to."

"Excuse me again, Ms. Kenyara "Although Julie was now holding her head up and looking around the room, Warren still spoke at the same time he raised his hand.

"Yes Warren. And you can just call me Julie."

"Well, I appreciate that, ma'am, considering you're a published author and all." Warren tried to cover up the intended sarcasm with sincerity. "What about self-publishing? Wouldn't it be more feasible for those of us without college degrees to self-publish? But that runs into the problem of hiring a publicist that most of us can't afford, doesn't it?"

"I was going to get to the issue of self-publication in just a minute if you'll bear with me." Julie looked back down at the floor and tried to regain her concentration.

"Oh, I'm sorry, Julie. I guess I'm just jumping ahead a little too much."

"That's perfectly alright."

The rest of the class was now aware of the tension. Most knew Warren and now knew what he was up to. Most would've asked questions that put Julie at ease. Watching her was becoming torture. The shakiness of her voice alone made others embarrassed for her. Oscar was in the class, and he liked Warren, but he also liked it when everyone got along. This writer's group, like several of the others was Oscar's second family. Some of the people he even got together with through the course of the year to party, watch a game, or go fishing. He knew Warren was a big boy and could take care of himself.

"Umm, excuse me, Julie," Julie looked quickly toward Oscar as if expecting more flack. "Why might the smaller presses be appropriate for some of our work?" Oscar knew Warren was looking at him, but they would talk about it half-jokingly later, like they always did.

"Well, sometimes the smaller presses take on smaller and experimental works. Like a collection of short stories." Julie didn't know if Oscar's question was sincere or not, but she welcomed it to get her back on track. Warren settled in his seat for the rest of the class, glaring at Oscar every time he set up interference to help Julie.

When lunch came, people paired or grouped together and drove off to various restaurants or delis. Few stayed in the lobby of the main dorm or returned to their rooms to snack on peanut butter and crackers. But this was really the first day of the conference; people still had a few bucks, and no one had received a critique of their project yet, so most felt good, adventurous, and wanted to meet new people. Even a lot of those that attended years prior and should know what to expect, felt that this year they got it right. Their stories flowed well with a strong voice, interesting characters and it was more compelling than it was the year before, because their wives, husbands, boyfriends, girlfriends, sons, and daughters told them it was. Those in their monthly writing groups may have thought it needed more work, but they were just jealous.

Jim, Warren, Oscar, Dorothy, and the clinical therapist from Tom Finnigan's group, Katrina, all went out to eat, traveling in Dorothy's SUV. It was a 99' black Chevy Blazer but looked on the inside and out as if it just rolled off the assembly line. She had just over 41,000 miles on it, but was blaming the majority of that on her stepdaughter.

"That girl, now that she's dropped out of college, she spends her whole time running around with her friends gettin' high. And I know she's gettin' high; cause I found a roach in my ash tray of all places. You wonder how she could be so stupid. Not only leaving it in her parent's car, but in a parent's car that happens to be a cop." Oscar and Warren laughed. They were sitting in the back seat along with Jim. Katrina was sitting in the bucket passenger seat in the front and looked at Dorothy concerned.

"What'd ya do?"

"The only thing I could do when you have a stepchild that hates you. I asked her if she could get me a bag." The guys in the back started laughing. Katrina was cautious at first but then joined in the chorus.

"You're kidding, right?" Katrina said, still laughing.

"No, it was some of the best weed my husband

and I ever smoked. Better than anything we ever confiscated at the police post." Katrina stopped laughing and looked even more surprised.

They pulled in at the Peppermill, a popular BBQ joint. The inside was more like an old mom and pop store, with retro 1960s tile and paneling. The row of shelves was replaced with high wooden tables and round bar stools. There were three booths on one wall that were seemingly out of place, as if from another restaurant. And there was a long table that could seat six, average height, again out of place but perfect for the five writers. They ordered a mix of short ribs, chicken wings, and some barbecue sandwiches made of turkey, pork, and beef, which they cut into squares so everyone could have a sample. They already started their meal by reaching over each other and across the table. Katrina was being polite by asking somebody to pass this or that. Dorothy filled her in.

"Honey, save your manners for when you take the agents and editors out to dinner. You're with writers now. You'll starve to death if you keep saying please and thank you."

"Yeah, that's what we call empty dialogue. You know, like when you write a query letter and you're trying to show an agent how gracious you can be." Jim was interrupted by the cell phone he had clipped to his belt. "Hallo."

"That's probably Julie saying that she's leaving."

Oscar tried to keep a straight face after he said it but broke into a smile when he looked at Warren. Warren looked at him steadily across the table for a couple of seconds.

"You've got barbeque sauce on your cheek." Oscar wiped his face, and Jim got up and walked away from the table for better reception.

Looking back and forth between Warren and Oscar, Dorothy asked, "What's this Julie thing all about? What did you guys do now?" Dorothy remembered two years ago when they had a famous author attend the conference and give classes. He brought an entourage with him, which Red Creek had to house. The entourage was one girl and three guys, though no one was completely sure which was which. They were cross-dressing and spoke in high, bored, and exaggerated manners. But everyone gladly made accommodations for them, thinking that the extra inconvenience would be worth the trouble. The author's arrogance, however, far exceeded his expertise. Two days into the conference, Oscar, Warren, and Jim, along with a few other attendees at the time, made up a barrage of elementary questions that made class discussion intolerable. They all kept a poker face as if they expected a serious answer, shunned the author at lunches and dinners, and when he offered to take a few of them to a local theater production, the writers made up other plans. The famous author (hint: a mystery writer) left early, mentioning something in an uncontrolled voice about the ignorance of the group, huffing out of the main dorm, never receiving his fees for breaking the tutorial agreement. The evening after, all the writers celebrated in the main dorm by drinking, mocking the authors books, reciting passages in melodramatic tones and giving outrageous reviews as if they were critics for the New York Book Review.

"Oh, nothing really. Warren just decided he didn't like the new golden child, so he started busting her chops." Sitting next to him, Dorothy slapped Warren on the arm with the back of her hand and had hardly any energy.

"You should be ashamed of yourself. She seems like a nice girl."

"Yeah, well, this nice…" Jim dropped back in his chair looking bewildered. "What is it?" Katrina was the first to deliver.

"That was Bobbie on the phone. Ahh…You know that writer from Wisconsin that hasn't shown up yet?" No one said anything, they didn't need to, having made a mental note of who was at the conference and who wasn't. If they didn't know them from previous conferences, they tried to pair them up with the titles of the manuscripts that were on the list.

"Well, Bobbie got ahold of his family, and

apparently he died in a car crash in Illinois on his way down here for the conference."

"No," Dorothy was able to release, having just taken a bite from the barbeque pork sandwich.

"Wow, what a." Oscar felt he should say something but didn't know what. "That's terrible."

"To say the least."

Everyone stared for a minute, then slowly started eating or taking a sip from their drink. Wanting to occupy themselves for lack of having anything to say about the guy because no one ever met him. Then Katrina broke the silence while looking around the table.

"Was he the one on the handout that had the manuscript <u>Open Graves</u>?"

"Yeah, he was," Jim answered.

"That's a really curious title. I would like to have heard what it was about."

"I know. I thought that was an interesting title when I saw it in the paper. I was waiting to ask the guy when he got here what it was all about," Dorothy added. Warren leaned back in his chair, wiped the corners of his mouth, and looked at Jim.

"This may not be the best time to ask, but do you think I could have his room?" Everyone started laughing, even Dorothy, who hit Warren on the arm again. "What? Jim and Bobbie put him in the quiet dorm, and I've got some serious writing to do."

"You never have any serious writing to do," Oscar said, struggling through laughter and food.

Jim didn't attend any of the afternoon classes but instead printed up a message that he slid under the doors of all the rooms. It simply read: "Unscheduled, mandatory meeting in the main dorm (dorm F) at 8 PM for all Red River Writers." Jim also put it on the bulletin board in case some of the attendees didn't return to their rooms before then. In the meantime, Elaine Lukeman, a popular author of regional short stories, was giving a class on approaching agents and editors. This being by far the most attended class of the afternoon, Tom Finnigan's class on "Trying to find time to write", and Buzz Snyders class on "How to break the writer's block", carried only two to three participants. And because of the poor turnout, they both ended class early.

ello everyone. For those who don't know me, my name is Elaine Lukeman. I have been fortunate enough to attend Red Creek Writers conferences now for." She thought for a moment, glancing at the ceiling and said, "Well, this is my sixth year. I missed one year after having my first collection of short stories published. So actually, seven years ago, I started coming here."

Elaine was a tall, slender woman with grace and style, being the actual epitome of the cliche. When she talked, she did it with her long delicate hands, seldom pulling her arms from her side. Her fingers were poetic in their movement, often drawing attention away from her face. In her mid-fifties, poised with patience, proper etiquette, and the posture of the royal family, but none-the-less approachable and comforting. She had dark hair and has yet to show any obvious gray. She taught creative writing at a community college in Mississippi, and her husband taught anthropology at a nearby university. Her credentials and talent would warrant her a more prestigious position almost anywhere, but she liked the pace and people where she is, helping young people and even older students that wanted to "better themselves", as society taught them to say. Besides, this gave her the freedom to raise her family and write the stories that she genuinely loved. Many at the conference had a great deal of respect for her.

Elaine started her career and life for that matter, late. She suffered depression in high school and then in college, having to drop out. Her family became impatient with her, defining her as unambitious, bored, and boring. She isolated herself locking herself away from the rest of the world. She would stare in a mirror for hours trying to evaluate her problem, but only becoming more and more sick and disgusted of who she was. Knowing that if she tried getting help, her family would only say that it was a desperate attempt for attention. Suicide was the only alternative. Today she jokes about it saying, "if my father wasn't such a lousy plumber, I'd be dead right now." She cut her wrists, in repairable fashion, while in the bathtub with the water running, thinking that the excess water would run out the overflow drain. Well, her father never hooked up the overflow drain. The water ran over the top of the tub just after

Elaine passed out, along the floor and out into the hallway. Her younger sister stepped into the bloody water when coming out of her bedroom.

In the weeks to follow, Elaine was forced to sit in on sessions of group therapy with other disturbed youths. One was her future husband. They both had a laconic sense about themselves in those days, and behind the counselor and backs of the other patients, they would often ridicule and imitate, sharing the same sense of humor. With the support and eventual love of each other, they worked their way through odd jobs, bad apartments, and finally college degrees.

"Some of you may remember that I gave this same class two years ago. And in those two years, the market has become increasingly difficult to get into. A lot of agencies have switched their attention more than ever to nonfiction material. Does anyone want to take a guess why?"

"Because no one can figure out how to do a goddamn thing on their own without referring to a manual." Warren's restless and abrupt tone got a few laughs in the room. Elaine smiled at Warren.

"That's a big part of it, Warren. More and more products are being created, so there are more and more instructions and more and more services."

"I meant that people are just becoming too stupid with books on how to raise their children, fix a leaky faucet, eat all they want without gaining weight…

how to date, and make money by doing nothing." A couple of the new people who also attended the morning class with Warren were of the thought that this was going to be a repeat of the same and shifted uncomfortably in their seats. But it was hardly going to be the same. Elaine and Warren knew each other well, and Elaine welcomed all of his input, also knowing that he would pace himself.

"Well, I surely can't argue with you. And that really is a good point. Adding to that would be the increase in college attendance. With that increase as well as the increase in trade schools, specialists are being looked at to provide material that can be bought in large quantities and circulated in academics." Elaine steered the discussion away from malice toward the nonfiction writer, knowing a couple were in class. The picture that she started out painting for the class seemed bleak for fiction writers, suggesting the internet, as well as think tanks of writers in Hollywood dominating the market of storytelling, although largely redundant. But Elaine reinvigorated everyone with the belief and her "faith" that the novel is soon going to make a comeback, just in time when most participants at the conference would be putting the final touches on their stories. Her passion was earnest and uplifting. She could've been Moses, but she was raised southern Baptist. There was no praising the Lord when the session was over, but no one was in a hurry to leave the church, wanting to talk with Elaine or among themselves about the future and their expectations.

Dinner came the way that lunch time did, with most everyone still wanting to get together and participate in the community and society of other writers, talking of the day's events and schedule for the rest of the week, even sneaking in bits of gossip for and about veteran attendees. Liz and Beverly took Tom to dinner and a few drinks to pick his brain. Lenny Garring took Noah Petermann, wanting to hear about his World War two experiences. But while they were in the parking lot, Joey Goode and Grace invited themselves to go along, often redirecting the topics at lunch toward pop culture, which eventually annoyed Lenny to the point that he asked Grace if she could "please let Noah finish."

Warren invited Katrina, but she said she was tired and wanted to lay down for a while. Standing nearby in the main dorm, Buzz Snyder volunteered to take her place, then upon seeing Elaine, Warren invited her as well. She graciously accepted, and that was the max that Warren could take in his old four-wheel drive Ford pickup with the stick on the floor. Unless of course somebody wanted to ride in the bed of the truck.

Warren's attire matched the frayed and worn seating of the truck. Buzz had on jeans a checkered button shirt, tennis shoes and a wind breaker, while Elaine was dressed in a knee length patterned skirt, with a long sleeve button blouse, knitted shawl, and black pumps. Buzz was going to sit in the middle so Elaine could avoid any embarrassing situation that straddling the stick shift might cause, but she insisted on climbing into the cab of the truck first. She spread her legs and pulled her skirt back, so it was above her knees and out of the way. Both she and Warren seemed completely comfortable with the seating arrangements while Buzz couldn't stop glancing over at the both of them thinking how peculiar they looked.

"So, where do ya all wanna go," Warren belted. His voice more upbeat than it was earlier in the day. Elaine smiled, raised her eyebrows, and looked back and forth between the two men. They both looked as though they were going to leave it up to her. So, she replied.

"How does Denny's sound?"

"Great."

"Sounds good to me."

Warren's truck had wide winter tires. He got them cheap, so obviously he couldn't turn down the deal, although they were very unconventional, especially year-round where he lived. They caused a loud hum when driving on pavement. Coupled with a muffler that had a few rusted holes in it, conversation in the cab was almost done at a yell, even in the city driving.

"So, what's with this meeting? Does anyone know?" Elaine heard Buzz, but it didn't come through clearly to Warren.

"What's that?" Not sure if Buzz heard Warren, Elaine interjected. "He asked what the meeting was about."

"Apparently Jim's getting everybody together to find out about what should be done for the attendee that died in that car crash on his way to the conference." Both Elaine and Buzz looked surprised. Warren glanced over at them.

"Oh, you all probably haven't heard yet." Elaine shook her head. "The guy from Wisconsin died yesterday on his drive down. Jim just wants everyone's input on what the Red Rivers should do…you know, like send flowers, write a letter…something like that."

"Whose group was he in?" Trying to make it so Warren and Buzz could hear her, Elaine looked straight ahead when she spoke, raising her voice just enough above the noise.

"Joey Goode's." Warren could tell that Buzz didn't hear him, so he repeated it. "Joey Goode's."

"So, he wrote literary?" Buzz added. Warren nodded his head. They all were silent for a couple minutes, then Elaine broke in.

"Is he the one that wrote <u>Open Graves</u>?" Warren nodded again. "That's an interesting title. I wonder what it's about." Warren shrugged, and Buzz shook his head, raising his eyebrows with a tight smile.

When they arrived at Denny's, Warren parked his truck diagonally across two spaces as though he had an expensive European sports car that he didn't want anyone else parking next to. Buzz thought it was odd but didn't question it, and Elaine seemed unaffected by Warren's eccentricities. It was still just a little early for the evening crowd, so seating was sparse with several open tables and booths, yet the restaurant had their "please wait to be seated" sign up.

"Three?" A young girl, in her early twenties with braided pig tails, approached, grabbing menus from a slot in front of the cash register.

"Yes."

"Smoking or non?"

"Smoking," Elaine cut in, then looked around at Buzz. "Is that alright?"

"Yeah, that's fine with me, Elaine. I just didn't know you were a smoker." She had been trying to quit for years. Her husband won't let her smoke in the house, so she goes to the bathroom a lot. Her excuse is age and that her bladder control isn't what it used to be. He recommended that she go see a doctor, but she's hoping that she can kick the habit before he makes her see a doctor. The three sat down in a booth by a window. Buzz and Elaine sat on the same side with their backs toward the direction they came in. Warren sat opposite. He barely looked at the menu, knowing what he wanted and what he always gets at Denny's.

"I think I'm gonna get the meat loaf and mash potato platter."

In an inside aisle booth seat, back toward the entrance in the nonsmoking section, Warren noticed Julie. She was sitting by herself. Warren didn't say anything but studied her while Elaine and Buzz were talking over what to order. He could tell that she noticed him, all three of them, but was pretending she didn't, trying to look as though she was too consumed in studying the objects at her table. As if everything were a newfound discovery. She hadn't received her food yet, so she had to try and look busy. Lucky for her, she brought her laptop into the restaurant. She had been working on her manuscript earlier but wrote twelve pages and ran into a block where she was going to take her main character next. That was largely the reason she left the campus to eat. She really wasn't that hungry, but she knew she would be soon, and she thought getting out for a while might stir her creativity.

Initially Warren wanted Julie to see him looking at her, then act unresponsive, to tease or test her and see if she'd have the courage to come over and say hi. He wanted her to be more than aware of his discontent for her success, but it wasn't just the success; he was bitter toward the fortunate breaks she had in life and bitter toward her people, her race, though he'd never admit it, and it would probably only come out in some sort of psychotherapy that Warren would never commit himself to. But Warren was seeing something awkward and childlike in her mannerisms. It looked as though she has hardly developed into an adult. Her nervousness made Warren realize that she had never been exposed to any conflict in her life, or very little at all. Not like he was. What would she do if she saw the things that he saw? Where would she be? Could she handle it? Would

she be a better or worse person? He could see her protected upbringing and the constant push that her professional mother and father gave her to succeed. He got up from the table and walked towards her.

7

Warren walked past Julie, and when she could see him near the side of her vision, she pretended to be more focused. Again, he saw through her behavior and went into the restroom. While he was gone, the waitress took Buzz and Elaine's order. Elaine also ordered for Warren. When Warren came back through, he touched Julie on the shoulder. She jumped.

"Oh, you surprised me. I didn't see you come in." The jump was real, but her acting was poor. She had one hand to her chest as if settling her heart rate. "It's Warren, isn't it?"

"Yeah. Would you like to come join us?" She pretended to look as though she never saw where they were sitting.

"Ahh…yeah, sure. If that's alright?"

"I wouldn't be askin' if it wasn't." Julie had to look and see if Warren was just being funny or impatient with her. He smiled and she joined them for dinner, slightly apprehensive for a moment when she realized they were sitting in the smoking section but braved the unhealthy element to fit in and try and make her time at the conference more comfortable. Warren didn't speak much to her during the meal, but he didn't speak much to anyone. However, Elaine always had the right question or statement to keep things interesting or to avoid those awkward silences. And Buzz wasn't without energy either, wanting to know more about Julie.

Everyone got the message to attend the meeting, and everyone did except for Warren and Joey. Warren knew what it was about and knew where it would probably end up. The group would decide to send flowers. But that's the reason he didn't want to attend. It would be kinder not to do anything, avoid it, stay away. Let those that knew him to suffer silently and to pace themselves. The grieving don't want to deal with superficial gestures. This is the way Warren felt. Joey was meeting with family that lived in the area.

Everyone was talking in much softer voices than they were the night before because rumor traveled. Everyone asked for details, but there were none. The writer died in the car crash.

"May I have everyone's attention please?" Jim worked his way toward the center of the room. "Well, most of you already have a pretty good idea why I called this meeting and for those of you still wondering, here it is. One of our fellow writers that was supposed to attend the conference was killed in an auto accident driving down here from Wisconsin." There was no sound. No sighs, or gasps, which made Jim think that everyone already knew.

"Was he published?" Jeff Hermann asked without the intent that it mattered, but it came out like most everything he said. Mostly uncensored. Jim looked at him puzzled as if wanting to say something offensive or maybe defensive, but so many others gave the same look that Jim didn't bother. Grace did, however.

"No dear, he was just another miserable wannabee like the rest of us who'll be lucky to get his obituary in print."

"C'mon, I didn't mean anything by it. I was just curious."

"I called the meeting because I wanted to get some feedback on what, or if, we should do for the family. Initially, I thought about sending flowers, but that seemed sort of cliche to me, and I was hoping someone may have a better idea." Jim raised his eyebrows and looked around. "And there it is. I don't know, maybe we should just return the money and enclose a letter offering Red Creek Writers condolences and leave it at that." Jim looked around again. "Any ideas?"

May Burkstrom was sitting in one of the cushioned

chairs that were lined against the big windows so a person could look out into the square between the four adjoining dorms. Katrina was sitting on one arm of the chair while Elaine was sitting on another. At seventy-three, this was May's third year attending the conference. Arthritis has crippled her hands to the point where she can only rely on her index fingers to type. Her hands are knotted and distorted, looking like the ends of a broken tree branch, where the wood has weakened and turned to punk. Her knees suffered the same malady and looked extremely worse, but were always covered by her pants. The inflammation of her joints caused her to walk with a cane, twisting her feet outward like Charlie Chaplin, and rocking with the same gait, though slower, much slower.

May lived in Boston, born, troubled, and will probably die there. Her husband died there, leaving her with nothing, not even good memories. She collected social security, lived on the second floor in a fair apartment, in a fair neighborhood, considering her income, and that she lived in the city. She rocked her way to church, to the market and to the bus stop or train station if she wanted to go further. And that's how she got here, by train, alone and on time, sitting in the same seat for two days hugging her purse and manuscript, that was hole punched and bounded with piercing pain. But hardly as painful as the story she wrote, a love story about a young girl still in high school right after World War Two that falls in love with an army sergeant, wounded and back from the war, recuperating and finishing his enlistment state side, before returning home to his wife and six-year-old daughter in Minnesota.

"Excuse me, Jim."

"Yes May."

"What story did he write?" The question didn't seem all that unreasonable. Especially being delivered in Mays soft voice. Not only that, but in order to hear, the crowd stirred less. However, Jim was failing to see why it was so important on what this fucking guy wrote. But this was what May asking this time, so Jim held his frustration.

"Uh, he wrote 'Open Graves'."

"Does anyone know what it's about?"

Jim took a deep breath, "Well, he was signed on with Joey's group and because he registered late for the conference, I'm pretty sure Joey hasn't got a chance to review it, but I'm assuming he sent along a synopsis. So, I'm sure when he gets back here, he'd love to share with anyone."

"Maybe we should send his family some Red Creek T-shirts." This was Abigail, of middle age and a self-professed witch (as if there were any others). No one knew much about her except that everyone expected her to be a lesbian and that she never had anything published but showed up with a different inspirational style manuscript for wiccans every year, which she talked about in vague and profound terms but never let anyone see. At first, it was thought that she was using the conference as a retreat, much like Noah, just to get some writing done and maybe make voodoo dolls, as some of the attendees liked to joke. But she was always seen about, walking in and out of dorms talking small talk with anyone and everyone, though rarely joining in dinner outings or evening drinks in the main dorm. She was always able to change the conversation when someone started asking about her. She wore dark, lose and one-piece dresses, jade, or silver sculpted jewelry, and always had a faint smell of ben-gay about her.

"T-shirts?" Oscar's voice was high-pitched when it came through and obviously disbelieving. A couple others laughed. "Abigail, please. Why would you say that?"

"I said it to draw him out." Everyone looked at her stranger than usual. "He's here, you know."

"Yeah, and so are the Marxs Brothers and Winston Churchill." Jim never had the patience for Abigail. A few more people laughed. Abigail, who was by one of the exits, stepped in front of two other writers and toward the center of the room.

"He's in this room right now. I know all of you think it's silly and you don't believe me, but it's true." Abigail had muscle damage done to one of her eyes when she was young, so when she looked at someone, if there was someone else standing close to them, it was hard to tell who she was looking at. She had her gaze fixed on Buzz or Jim, who happened to be standing next to each other, but neither one could tell who she was looking at. Jim's a very practical man and approaches everything with a degree of skepticism, but he's also understanding and sometimes listens to others to a fault. Besides, no one could deny her the chance to talk. Not only because she was a returning member, but because, although she was allusive, she still had no problem getting in anybody's face. She often came in too close when she talked, and as many have said before, it felt kinda creepy.

"Okay, if he is here, why is he here of all places?"

"He has unfinished business." Abigail said it abruptly and hard, then looked around the room, with both eyes. She was in a spiritual moment, unaffected by the scrutiny that everyone was giving her. Her body is short and heavy set–not obese, but with definite rolls. Her thin, dark, and draping dress showed her contours easily, plus the fact that she didn't have on any underwear. She kept her hair short and spiked; another joke was that it wouldn't fall down into the cauldron as she mixed potions of bat tongues and lizard tails.

"What's his business?" Oscar looked serious and attentive, like a child listening to story hour.

Abigail stared at him and the television stand that was next to him for a moment. It built suspense in the room, evident by the silence.

"The same thing that everyone else here wants… to be published."

"Not a problem. Ghostwriters get published all the time." Liz and Beverly laughed immediately to Tom's line, with several others joining in the chorus.

"No kidding, look at all the celebrity bio's out there." Lenny couldn't help saying that with a great deal of contempt. Every chance he got; he was going to slander books on celebrities. He felt the writing was generally garbage, they whined too much, were taking all the good agents, and were eating up the market for real struggling writers that don't have the means and access the famous do.

For a few seconds, Abigail looked confused, but then wove her way back into the ranks as the banter caused random jokes and more laughter. Jim eventually settled the crowd down to get a few more suggestions, some of which were smart-ass replies but a few serious ones. He ended the meeting by asking everyone to think about it during the week and, if they came up with any good ideas, to let him know. At the end of the week, they would have another meeting and decide what to do.

Jim and Oscar made a liquor run that evening, bringing back a few requests and Jim's own taste (Oscar didn't drink), and setting everything on the table in the main dorm. Joan had them buy her a pint of rum and some coke. The War Correspondent had to have his brandy, while Dorothy and Grace went in together on a twelve pack of Bud Light.

Although Oscar had to quit drinking several years ago, he liked to see others having a good time, so he bought an extra twelve to put in the fridge and a fifth of Black Velvet for shots, which he liked when he was drinking.

"You never did tell me, Oscar, why'd you quit drinking?" Jim and Oscar kept very little from each other. For that matter, most everyone who has attended the conference for several years, except, of course, for Abigail, has poured out a great deal of intimate details about themselves, but there are so many details from year to year, that a lot is left untold.

"DUI man, DUI" Dorothy was sitting at the table when Jim asked. "What'd they give ya in Missouri for that?"

"They gave me time served with community service and pulled my license for a year."

"That's about what you'd get in Kansas," said Dorothy.

"So, you quit drinking just because of the DUI?" Jim asked, almost letting the topic go, but the question slipped by before he thought of anything else.

"No, not really. There's more to it than that." It was obvious that Oscar was becoming a little uneasy; he was stretching in his chair, scratching the back of his head, and avoiding eye contact. Jim just finished putting the beer in the fridge and mixing himself a gin and seven. He and Dorothy gave each other concerned glances, both knowing that they had touched a nerve. For both curiosity and care for his friend, Jim pried.

"What is it, Oscar, you're like the Iceman Cometh?" Jim pointed toward the fridge. "You buy booze for your old drinking buddies, don't touch a drop, and now there's this big mystery." Turning sideways in his chair, Oscar leaned forward, putting his elbows on his knees, and rubbed his hands together.

"I'm a little more like the Iceman than you think." The first thing that came to Dorothy's thoughts was Oscar's wife at home, lying dead and stuffed in a closet. Then she saw herself helping local police escort Oscar away in handcuffs. "Okay, honey, you're scaring me a little bit here."

"Oh, no, it's not like that.", Oscar took a relaxing breathe. "I started getting into this habit of going out drinking every night after I got off my shift at the hospital. And being that we were understaffed, I was putting in a lot of over time. Plus, they had me working in the ER then. As you can well imagine, the drinking brought me down from this hyper state I was in, accelerated by the speed I was taking to help me get through the day. I also took on the overtime because Sonya and I were having a hard time trying to keep up with putting Emily through college.

To make a long story short, I will keep myself from trying to turn this into an excuse. One night, when I got home after quite a few drinks, Sonya and I got into a big argument. We never really got into an argument before, and while it was happening, I think it even surprised the both of us. Anyway, at some point, Sonya started throwing things at me, grabbing little statues and candles off the shelves. You know, shit like that. I worked my way toward her, wanting to get her to stop." Oscar was watching it all unfold again and was raising his hands up as if reenacting the scene to see where he went wrong. "She had this anniversary plate in her hand. I remember putting my hand up to block her swing, but couldn't catch her in time, and she hit me with right on the bridge of my nose. The pain just shot right through me. When I hit her, I didn't even think that I was hit her. It was like a reflex swinging at something that caused pain. It was sudden, with the back of my hand.

She fell to the floor and lay there in terror, holding the side of her face. And she was giving me this look that I can't forget." Oscar's voice was still steady, as though he had to tell the story before or wanted to tell it before, if to come to some sort of resolution or to tell it himself. But tears were seeping into his eyes. "When I realized what I'd done, I started apologizing. And when I went to help her up, she ran into the bedroom and locked herself in. I pleaded with her by the door, for I don't know how long. Not knowing what else to do, I decided to go for a drive in the car to think things out. Well, that was another stupid move, because that same night I got pulled over for speeding. And when the cops came up to the car, right away they could tell I'd been drinking. So ever since then, I haven't touched a drop."

Dorothy had seen a lot of domestic disputes. It was the biggest part of the job. She'd seen too many battered wives and their husbands crying, even pleading they'd never do it again. It was usually a lie though, returning the following week to hand cuff and put the husband in the back of the cruiser. She had also seen the effects of psychological abuse. Oscar was a good man, and Dorothy knew it. He was the type who would be over penalized for the slightest mistake. Good guys like him usually are. Oscar was the opposite of abusive, letting things torment him to the point that he'd sacrifice everything to make it right. But Oscar looked physically threatening. A healthy, strong black man with rough and dominant facial features. As a nurse, patients heart rates were sometimes monitored. If they hadn't met Oscar prior, sometimes their rhythm would oscillate in rapid waves as soon as he entered the room, but in the long run he had a much more calming effect on them because they found security in his calm and strength, knowing they could count on him to lift and carry them if need be. He was naturally athletic, and even when he was drinking, any free time he had to join in a sport or local team, he would.

"Honey, I'm sure Sonya looks back on it now and really sees what a mistake it was." Dorothy didn't believe her own words, because she felt that Sonya was probably milking the situation as much as she could. She met Sonya the first year she attended the conference and didn't like her. On the other side of domestic abuse, Dorothy saw a lot of women that exaggerated their husband's behavior. Some that got a certain thrill out of some level of abuse, knowing it would get them pampered treatment for a while. Dorothy felt that Sonya was somewhere in that echelon of women, playing games to get more than she really deserved and taking advantage of Oscar's good nature.

"Hey, it's the squirrel hunter." That was a nickname Jim had for Warren. Warren went to the fridge and grabbed a beer as if he had bought it himself, then sat down at the table.

"I've heard you say that before. Why do you call him the squirrel hunter?" Dorothy meant to ask several times before, but it seemed she was always interrupted. Jim looked over at Warren.

"What was it, four years ago, maybe?" Warren shrugged his shoulders barely interested. "Well, anyway we were sitting around this table drinking. There was Warren, me, and Jarvis Atkins." Jim looked over at Oscar. "You remember Jarvis?"

"How could I forget. He stole one of my ideas and got published."

"Yeah, but it didn't sell very well. Plus, it was terrible writing." Jim assured Oscar, smiling, and hoping to get the same response, but Oscar was still bitter about that. Jim knew that Dorothy didn't know Jarvis, because that was the last year he attended and Dorothy started coming to the conference three years ago. Jim continued his story looking primarily at Dorothy.

"Well Jarvis quit coming the year before you arrived. The three of us were sitting around bull shitting and somehow got on the subject of Vietnam. Jarvis and Warren started sharing a few stories, which got me a little curious, so I started asking some questions. We got on the subject of movies made about the war. One of my favorites has always been <u>The Deer Hunter</u>."

"Oh yeah, I like that one too, especially in the beginning—the wedding scene." Dorothy sounded excited as if she were talking about the Wizard of Oz. Warren was showing complete disinterest in the conversation and looking across the room at Elaine, Julie, and Joan. They were sitting in the lounge chairs and talking about something that seemed far more interesting, as they would keep throwing their heads back in laughter. Jim and the others seemed used to Warren becoming disconnected with topics that he didn't want to be a part of, continuing as if he weren't there, but Warren always listened to every word, interjecting when he felt it was really important.

"Anyway, I asked naively if there were any scenes in that movie that he could relate to. He said no, he has never been deer hunting. Not only that, but he also said he never saw the movie." Dorothy looked over at Warren in disbelief. "But he did tell me that he always hunted small game with his daddy before he went in the service, and that if he wasted any shots, his daddy would smack him. So just like Robert DeNiro, take his game out with one shot. So, you always got your squirrel, didn't ya Warren?"

"No, actually I got smacked quite a bit. And I didn't get any better when I was over there either. If I saw any ferns move, I'd just close my eyes and pull the trigger until I emptied my clip." Warren made light of it. Dorothy and Oscar laughed politely but didn't want to ask the same questions that Jim did. It was something still ingrained in the back of their minds the way it was three decades ago. That Vietnam was a taboo subject for all veterans, and it shouldn't be discussed flippantly or so openly, like Jim had no problem doing. The truth is, Warren didn't care anymore; it was boring for him. He was in the thick of it with a forward recon unit and saw horrific sights, but it seemed like another life to him now. He became tired long ago of trying to get recognition, or respect for what he had to go through. And when it did finally come, it was too late, plus it didn't seem heartfelt. When young people came up to him in later years and seemed in awe, as if what he went through was some sort of mysterious and secret journey that tested the boundaries of the mind, he could only laugh, because all it was to him was being in constant fear and having to adjust his attitude for every situation. He didn't feel any wiser because of it other than to stay away from it, and he didn't feel worldly as soon as he got home. He felt simpler for a time, that he couldn't have an open mind about things. He felt primitive.

The following day began with one coffee pot marked regular and the other decaf. However, it was still undetermined who was the first one to make it. It was suspected that the War Correspondent was the culprit, mostly because he seemed regimented, and everyone knew he was an early riser. They also knew that he drank decaf. Jim was out in the lobby again before anyone else, with his pink slippers, pajama bottoms and a T-shirt. Well, other than the mystery coffee maker, who was obviously already gone.

"Hum, alright, somebody was kind enough to label which one is which," Jim said out loud but to himself. He studied the handwriting on the pieces of paper for a minute to see if it looked familiar. He didn't recognize it. Julie came in from outside with sweats on. She had been jogging and it was 6:05.

"Good morning."

"Good morning. What the hell have you been doing?" It was less a question than an accusation. Julie started stretching in the middle of the lobby, in the center of the cushioned chairs.

"Just going for a little run before my class this morning. It helps to loosen me up."

"Your class isn't until nine o'clock."

"I'm an early riser." Julie was doing the splits and touched her crotch all the way to the floor. Jim couldn't help raising his eyebrows as Julie was looking away. Julie had all the right parts in the right places. She was slender and certainly agile. She had a nice face, not distinct, Jim thought. He felt she looked maybe too Japanese or too stereotypical. Others might say she was hot, but to Jim it seemed as though she had limited expression, as if trying to find pleasure in her face during sex would spoil the moment. However, seeing her spread her legs apart like that, and right after he woke up from a dream about his secretary back home, in which he was trying desperately to finish humping her (not that he ever did but wanted to for as long as she worked there), while listening to the husband running up the steps to the bedroom, he saw Julie in a different light. The lights of amateur porn where he'd walk up to her while she was on the floor, pull his dick out through the one snap fly in his pajamas, and let her suck him with such force that she'd have to squeeze his ass with one hand while wrapping the other around the base of his cock to steady his aim and could control his hips, so she could rock him back and forth with rapid and intense motion.

"Hey, what's everyone up to?" Jim jumped. Oscar came in from the door behind him. He asked the question as if he knew the kind of moment Jim was in. "Perhaps he saw me staring at her," Jim thought.

"Good morning," Julie said.

Oscar sat down by Jim and smiled.

"Asshole," Jim told Oscar, knowing that he had a pretty good idea what he was thinking.

"I see someone labeled the pots today."

"Yeah, but I still don't know who made it," Jim replied. "Hey Julie, did you make the coffee?"

"No, I don't drink coffee, but I would've been more than happy to make it," she said leaning over and talking into her knee as she was doing hurdlers stretch. Abigail entered. She had on another loose and flowing dress. She made large strides across the room toward Jim and Oscar, as if on a mission. Julie told her good morning as she passed by. Abigail only nodded her head rapidly with a tight smile, but any greeting from Abigail was a good sign. She sat down across the table from Jim and Oscar with her back toward Julie. She looked at Jim or

Oscar–it was hard to tell–and folded her arms on the table. "He's still here, at this very moment.

In this room."

"You mean the ghost, right?" Jim wanted to glance over at Oscar, but he knew if he did, they would both start to laugh. And it wasn't so much what Abigail said as the way she said it—fast, as if she were complaining about seeing cockroaches and expecting the landlord to take care of it.

"Yes, the writer is from Wisconsin." Abigail was from Allen Town Pennsylvania, where she read tarot cards and made potions for anyone that would take her more seriously, but rarely dealt with the spirits. When she did, it was usually for people that she was closer to or who had been coming to her for a long time. But in any town or city that suffered a great economic loss, you could find more businesses that offered services in alternative spiritual guidance. People wanted to believe that things were going to get better or at least see what the future had in store for them. And if it was dire, perhaps they could take steps to avoid it, unlike relying on a major corporation that seems utterly secure one minute and then closes shop the next, betraying their trust, before moving to another country. If Abigail could, she'd only specialize in potions, but her clients wanted other things, and she had to pay the bills, so anything that was remotely related to witchcraft, she pretended to be an authority in.

Abigail couldn't define it, but she felt this spirit

was too strong to ignore, otherwise she would say nothing, but go somewhere else where she couldn't feel it's presence. Or if she couldn't avoid it, she would change her aura with a special ceremony held in the quiet of her room late at night. This would make her unapproachable and less sensitive to the spirit's pain. She tried it however the night before with no success. Unfortunately for her, there were no potions that applied to the spirit realm. Potions effected only the living, the tangible, they could be concocted to alter the mind, but not the soul. That was one of the first lessons her grandmother taught her.

"We have to hold a group seance. I believe this is the best way that we can help this writer." She lied. She didn't care to help; she just wanted to get rid of the feeling. Jim decided to amuse her.

"Well, I can't really call the group together for that, Abigail. But I'm sure you'll get a lot of people to attend by word of mouth if you want to set a time, preferably in the evening after classes and dinner. I can't say that you'll get everyone to attend, but I'm sure you'll get a few. At least enough to bully this guy outta here."

"Just put a message on the board. That way, almost everyone will see it." Oscar surprised himself at how sincere he sounded. Julie heard the last part of the conversation and, not wanting to be pressured into joining, left the lobby quietly to go back to her room in the other dorm. Abigail knew that they were stroking her ego, but she was used to it. It was a big part of her life, and the only appropriate way to deal with it, she found, is to work with all the patronizing and use the best of it. She knew a message on the bulletin board would work. These were writers, they'd attend just for the experience or to write about it and mock it later. Nonetheless, just to show up would be the support she needed, even if everyone was skeptical. As long as one person could perform the ritual, the rest that were needed were just bodies.

"Yeah, you're right. Good idea. Thanks." Both Jim and Oscar said "you're welcome" simultaneously uncertain who she was looking at. Then looked at each other.

"I have to leave. This spirit is making me feel uncomfortable."

"That's very understandable," Jim replied.

"Besides, I have to get that notice typed up to put on the board. Would tonight be okay?"

"Sure." Jim thought for a second. "Actually, I think quite a few of the attendees were planning to go see a play tonight put on by the college. Tomorrow night might be better."

Abigail spoke without looking at anyone, thinking aloud. "Yes, yes, that would be better still. I need to get a hold of my grandmother first. It may take all of tonight. I better leave." She got up and paced out of the room with her head down, as if she were avoiding looking at something.

"What play was it that everyone was going to see?" Oscar asked. "Our Town. Wait a minute, I thought you were going."

"I am, just no one told me what it was. Aren't you going?"

"I thought about it, but I'm not really big on plays." Joan entered through the door that Abigail went out.

"Well, good mornin' all."

"Morning."

"I just bumped into Abby." Joan was the only one that called her that and the only one that every really talked to her. "What's this about a seance tomorrow night?"

"Yeah, she wants to get rid of our ghost writer. I told her that almost everyone is going to the play tonight. So, she's going to have it tomorrow night for anyone that wants to join in."

"Well, that sounds like more fun than that play. I'd give up the play for that."

"Apparently, she needs to get a hold of her grandma tonight anyway before she can do anything. Don't ask me what for."

"I thought her grandma was dead." Jim raised his eyebrows and Oscar squinted, automatically thinking of something practical.

"Maybe she means her other grandma."

"No, I'm pretty sure she's only talking about that one. You see, the rest of her family pretty much left her. From what I gathered in the little bit of time we spent together, her mother and father were put in prison when she was very young for armed robberies. I guess they mostly held up stores, and when they tried robbing a bank, they got caught. None of her other relatives would take her in."

"Okay, Joan, you know her better than the rest of us. Is she gay?"

"Oh Jim, what kind of question is that? What if she is? Are you gonna kick her out of the conference?"

"No, but I have a bet with these guys," he thumbed and nodded his head toward Oscar, "that's been going on for three years now, and I would like to see it settled."

"Well, if she is, she swings both ways because she has a sixteen-year-old daughter who's embarrassed of her and went to live with her father." There was quiet.

"So what classes are you guys going to this morning?"

10

Josslyn Albury came in through the door behind Oscar and Jim. She's the 26-year-old in Tom Finnigan's group. This is her first-year attending, wanting to write but not wanting to deal with people. She was shy, clumsy, and dumpy-looking, a girl that put on weight easily, then lost it just as fast, and dropping her shoulders when she walked. Her attire never stands out from her military field jacket, army boots to match, or wool cap. In the summertime if she has the chance, on a cool day, she'll wear the same. Her introverted behavior cost her a good education, hiding from answers and from excelling. She enjoys reading and does well at the bookstore. Studying people quietly all her life, she paired people with the kind of material they read. When the customers were looking for something and stumped, her quiet suggestions often moved them directly toward a book that suit their taste. If not for this, and the manager afraid to hurt her feelings, she would've been fired right away. Knocking over displays, tripping over cords into customers, accidently tipping a shelf of books through the store front window, would've sent anyone else packing. But Josslyn loved books and it showed. She worked in her Township library prior to the bookstore, but taxes weren't covering the cost of damage she was doing.

Josslyn idolized Franz Kafka, loved Kurt Vonnegut, and the first book she ever read was the <u>Martin Chronicles</u> by Ray Bradbury when she was six. She reviewed every periodical and book that Stephen Jay Gould ever wrote, adding to her sci-fi short stories an accuracy when describing educators at a prestigious university slowly mutating into snails or that Charles Darwin was actually a space alien set with false credentials and a bogus history in order to help accelerate human civilization because aliens monitoring the planet were getting bored. Josslyn was pushed and pressured into attending the conference by her family, knowing that she didn't belong in her conservative Indiana town. Besides, her mother and father were getting older, having three older children, but none, although they were all wilder than Josslyn, cost as much in repairs.

Josslyn's coat got caught in the door, with one of the bottom pockets somehow catching the outside knob, so she had to step back outside, unhook it, and come back in. When she did, everyone greeted her with good mornings. "Morning." Her voice was barely audible, but the trio noticed her lips move.

She sat down on the same side of the table as Joan, but near the other end, with a seat open between them. Joan is the only one she's really talked to since she's been there, other than Tom Finnigan, but that was forced upon her because she had to participate in the group.

"Want some coffee?" Oscar asked.

"Uh…sure" She didn't drink much coffee, but she was forcing herself to make attempts to fit in, and she almost wanted to with these people, which she currently didn't understand. She was feeling less that they were better than her, like she felt all her life with most people, and more like they were neither. Although she was raising out of her chair to go get a cup, Oscar was already out of his seat, being closest to the coffee pot.

"Stay there, hon, I'll get it." Josslyn didn't take any notice of it, because she figured it was the way he probably talked to all younger women, but Joan and Jim certainly did, looking at each other quickly. The only person they ever heard Oscar call "hon" was his wife. And as far as they knew, he didn't even call his daughter that. But they did hear him call her sweetie. They both thought it may have been an honest mistake because it came so easily and naturally.

"Regular or decaf?"

"Regular please?" Oscar sat the Styrofoam cup on the table in front of Josslyn. "Thank you."

"Anytime." Oscar smiled warmly. "Oh, and here ya go." He put a cup of sugar packets and some Carnation next to her. She said thanks again. Looking into Oscar's face, she reached for the sugar, knocking over her coffee with the sleeve of her coat. The coffee flowed across the table into copies of Joan's recent essays. Everyone stood up, Joan pulling her papers away too late, Jim pulling other things away from the spill, and Oscar taking a huge stride over to the table with the coffee pots to grab napkins.

"Oh, I'm soo sorry." Josslyn apologized profusely, mainly to Joan. "That's okay, dear. Don't worry about it."

"I'm such a klutz."

"It was just an accident. If you're worried about my essays, I'll just go back to my room and print some more copies. It's no big deal." But on Josslyn's face everyone could tell it was a big deal. Oscar walked around the table with some more napkins and started wiping in front of Josslyn. He noticed some splattered off the table, on the bottom of her coat and on her lap.

"Are you okay, hon? Did that burn you?" There it was again. Joan and Jim couldn't help talking to each other with their eyes. Josslyn was hurt; she felt the pain of the hot coffee, but the endurance of the humiliation made the sting bearable.

"No, I'm fine." They all finished cleaning up the mess. "I need to go back to my room and change." When Josslyn walked out of the dorm, she caught her coat on the door again. Jim wanted to ask Oscar something and Joan something along the same lines.

When Josslyn pulled off her pants in her room, the skin on her lap, and some spots on the inside of her legs were red and swollen. She had some Neosporin that she kept in a first aid kit wedged in her suitcase. It stung at first to try and rub it on. Feeling like a fool, especially catching her coat again on the way out, and the pain of the burn made her cry.

"God, I'm such an idiot." She clenched her teeth while sitting on the edge of the bed and continued to circulate the cream on her legs. After covering the entire area, she stepped back over to her suitcase and took out some Ultracets. She saved a few that she had to take after hurting her shoulder at work. She swallowed two, hoping that it would take less than an hour before they started working on the pain. She carefully changed her underwear and replaced her tampon, feeling clumsy, fat, and filthy. Josslyn didn't think she could go to a class that morning, but she needed to make the others believe that the coffee didn't really hurt her. And she wanted to just see Oscar again. He was so nice. Maybe he's like that with everyone she thought. She was sure he was married but didn't pay attention to the ring. He just seemed married; besides, even if he wasn't, she didn't think that he'd find her attractive.

"So, when did you start calling everyone, hon?" Jim figured he could be indiscreet with Joan there.

"What are you talking about?"

Warren entered the dorm with Barnell close behind him and talking, talking about something, and given the look on Warren's face, it was annoying and boring. Grace came out of her room at the same time, again with her cotton pajamas which gave no indication that she had on a bra or panties. Her long dark hair was combed through only with her fingers, disheveled, but on her it looked sexy, as if she just got out of bed after a romp with her lover. The first person she saw was Warren but noticing how intent his company was being in discussion, she lightly waved with a tired gesture and gave him a half smile. Warren only rolled his eyes to show how thrilled he was about his new friend. After receiving good mornings from Joan, Jim, and Oscar, the other three converged at the coffee pot table. Warren first poured Grace a cup then asked Barnell if he wanted some, hoping the gesture would get Barnell to change the topic or shut him up, but he only broke stride long enough to say, "no thank you, I don't drink coffee."

This was no surprise to Warren, thinking that if he did, he would be completely unbearable, plus it seemed fewer and fewer young people were drinking coffee these days, even with the popularity of Starbucks and all those college coffee houses. They wanted to drink soda pop in the morning.

"You see that a spirit, or the idea of a spirit's existence is utterly impossible. Schopenhauer totally dismissed it as nonsense." Everyone keyed in on Barnell's statement, giving him a curious stare. Realizing that everyone had heard, he froze. Warren decided to solve the mystery, although he would've rather let others take over the conversation, letting Barnell explain himself, which he seemed to thoroughly enjoy.

"We ran into Abigail in the other dorm. She invited us to a seance tomorrow night."

"Yeah, we know," Jim said.

"What's this?" Grace responded with a faint chuckle.

"She wants to have a seance for the guy from Wisconsin," Jim continued. "Does this mean his family won't get reimbursed if he shows up?"

This was Tuesday, and classes were dealing less with publishing and marketing and more directly with writing techniques. Joey Goode wanted to teach everyone how to write in southern dialect, but the greatest thing he liked about the class was that he got to do his mocking imitations of Mark Twain and William Faulkner novels. He always got laughs, even from a lot of old-timers who had heard the jokes before.

Denise Domikowski was able to give a class on narration. This was her chance as well to be humorous, speaking in different narrative voices, almost acting the parts out, but she used to do theater in local productions around the country, as well as dinner shows, and two commercials, so the demonstration was a welcomed challenge. Her upbeat nature always landed her roles in plays like Cheaper by the Dozen, The Importance of Being Ernest, and most Neil Simon adaptations. But when she tried to land a more serious role in The Crucible while living in Minneapolis, it went so badly that the casting director laughed himself to tears. However, always being the type that said her cup was half full, she turned the disaster into a book titled <u>When Good Actors Want To Play Bad Girls</u>. It was a compilation of her memoirs in various theater groups, filled with anecdotes about bad hair days and delightful upper middle-class insight that urban professionals like to keep on their coffee tables, along with books about apple blossoms and native birds. She felt that her book was such a hit that she intended to write another, more about her life and experiences since the first book, paralleling it with her childhood when she became one of the state finalists in the national spelling bee tournament. Little did she realize or want to know that the book did so well because of the way it was marketed, fooling readers into thinking it was another celebrity autobiography. The jacket listed her credentials as a theater actor, which is true, but upon first reading, one assumed that she is famous, or at least famous to some degree, but unknown only to that person. And the title itself was the genius product of her agent, who also happened to be in one of her acting troupes when they both were younger.

Denise tried to live her life by the scriptures of Oprah Winfrey and Martha Stewart. Her love life was similar with no noticeable or committed man in her life. She took charge and dominated most conversations. But increasingly with the success of her book and socializing more and more with the people she always aspired to be, she came to understand that there were others that could steal her thunder. And not only her thunder but could take away her rain. At conferences, she regained control of the storm. Hearing how hard it was to be published by veteran writers, who sometimes labored for years before anything was put in print and then were most often only recognized regionally, Denise mistook her fortune for talent. This was her second year at Red Creek Writers. Fresh and still a little naive last year, attendees found her charming.

This year, she was making demands. Her behavior was turning her into the celebrity she was confused for, and some of the attendees who knew her from last year were becoming impatient. New attendees accepted it as the eccentricities of being a published author and thought her Oprah Winfrey and Martha Steward babble was gospel.

When Warren was a boy, he would steal from the collection plate at the Baptist church his mother made him, and his two brothers go to. When the preacher found out he whipped Warren with his belt across the butt, lower back, and legs. The welts raised on his skin better than an eighth of an inch in many places. When he got home his father spanked him again. Warren decided to go to Denise's class that morning after considering another one of Julie's. If he would've gone to Julie's, he would've kept his mouth shut, just as a sort of apology. But the more he thought about it, the less he felt she deserved an apology. However, she didn't need to be given a hard time either, not at this conference anyway. He felt that she was going to become a real member, not just on paper, but a core member, returning in the years to come.

"I reckon I'd liken ta start ya'all with a story about dis here ghost upin' near Gordon's haller, when I wuz just an acorn sprout. My cousin and I be walkin' on home one-night affer we catch us a mess o' catfish outta Weller's pond. Dey wuz hardly any daylight lef, so's weez decided ta take a short cut through the haller, although are pappys done told us ta stay away fum dere time and time agin'." Denise was starting her class with an accent she used when doing a parody of Cat On A Hot Tin Roof. A Michigan writer rewrote the classic as a comedy and was able to get several small towns to put on the play, which local newspapers gave pleasant reviews to, calling Denise's performance "delightful." That was twenty years ago and since then, she felt she had a special ear for dialect. Warren was squinting his usually relaxed eyes.

"We'd just cross over a ridge n' were in the middle o' da flats when hear dis noise dat I never fa'get. Now, can anyone tell me what that narrative was told in?"

"Hee haw." Everyone laughed at Warren. He didn't know what the hell this lady was up to, but it better be good. Probably a good seventy percent of the people in class and attending the conference were from the south. Doing an imitation that sounded like Jim from Huckleberry Finn wouldn't win her many friends unless she had a very good excuse. Warren thought that if Bobbie were here, she'd probably exclude Denise from any future events with Red Creek Writers. Bobbie founded Red Creek, herself a published poet and regionally well-known with quite a few awards to compliment her style. Bobbie was raised in the hills of West Virginia at a time when people went through to film the squaller of impoverished and rural living in the south during the Kennedy administration. She knew how much of an insult it was to her mother and father then, making everyone look like slothful and ignorant hicks that came from the region. She also knew how much the portrayal hurt her family, friends, and relatives' chances for better jobs.

"That's very funny, but not the correct answer." Denise didn't seem embarrassed, and Warren was astonished by her insensitivity. "I used a character I created from one of my plays as a vehicle for narrating in the first person." She talked quickly without recognizing anyone around her, looking over the crowd and through them without any eye contact, giving every participant the sense that this class was going to be more complicated. Warren knew better.

"Now, is that a play that you wrote?"

"No this is a play that I acted in." Denise seemed surprised by the interruption. There was a pause and finally contacting Warren's eyes, she could tell he was unimpressed, but he was only one person in the class, and she learned long ago that it's more important to win favor with the majority and ignore the minority. So, she looked broadly around the room.

"Let me explain a little bit. I was to do theater."

"Did you do any Broadway?" Warren asked like an eager child.

"No, but I did act throughout the country in a great deal of prestigious productions." Oh my God did she actually say prestigious, Warren couldn't believe it.

Joan was just entering the main dorm. She missed the morning classes while trying to reprint her essays and didn't want to show up in the middle of the session. Tom Finnigan was going over the sample chapters that Liz and Beverly had given him. He normally did this in the privacy of his room, but the walls were starting to close in on him and he wanted to get out in the open for a little bit.

"Hello", Tom said in a sort of singsong nature, very upbeat and pleasing to Joan.

"Good morning."

"Not going to one of the classes this morning?"

"Well, I was going to, but I wanted to get something done." Tom saw Joan's manilla folder.

"Are those some more of your essays?"

"Yeah, Joey agreed to look at them during lunch today and give me his thoughts."

"Well, if they're anything like the ones that I

read last year, I'm sure you'll get a pleasing critique."

"Oh, I didn't know anyone else looked at them. I think I was a little braver then, leaving them out to read." Red Creek put two tables against the wall so published or unpublished authors could display their material for others in the group to read at their leisure. Tom smiled at Joan for a moment.

"I hardly think that it should take bravery on your part. You have a very authentic and beautiful voice that I think others should hear."

"Well, thank you." Joan couldn't believe it, she was blushing. Tom noticed it but noticed more. He noticed how the years made the outside of her eyelids drop in a way that caused her glances to look unintentionally sexy. She had a way of talking that caused her lips to move more than most, curling and rounding, preparing for a kiss. Tom thought how wonderful it would be to kiss them. They looked so soft and tender, but so creative. Joan took a banana off the top of the fridge and sat down at the table like the morning before.

"Are you giving a class this afternoon?" Years of modesty made changing the subject easy for her.

"No, I actually don't have another class until tomorrow. Are you going to the play this evening?"

"Oh yes. I'm going to take in all I can while I'm here. This is the only chance I get to spend an evening out." Joan just realized that it may have sounded like she was fishing for sympathy and hoped that Tom would just ignore it. Or maybe not, she wasn't certain.

"I know what you mean. My evenings out are usually spent picking up a video from Blockbuster and a bottle of wine." Joan knew he was lying just to be kind, so she smiled. Tom noticed a scratch and a bead of blood on the back of her hand as she was peeling the banana.

"What happened?" Tom pointed with concern. "Huh?"

"Your hand, it's bleeding."

"Oh, I must've hit against the desk in my room when I was trying to reposition my printer."

"Here, let me go get a band aid out of my room."

"No, that's al…" Before Joan could say any more, Tom was out of his chair and walking in long strides toward his room, the first one down the hall and just out of view of the main dorm. In barely more than the amount of time it took Joan to grab a napkin and dab the blood off the back of her hand, Tom returned with a Johnson & Johnson band aid that had images of Spider-Man on it. He sat down beside her.

"Here," he grabbed her hand delicately and laid it on the table, "put your hand flat." Joan noticed the superhero.

"Aren't I a lucky girl?" She paused. "I get to

wear Spider-man." She smiled. "Yeah, when I picked these up at the drug store, I wasn't paying attention, thinking that the cartoons on the box was just a sales gimmick. I didn't know they'd have them on the band aids. Besides, what better than a superhero for a super woman."

"This so-called super woman is getting old., spotty., thinning…and horrible skin." Joan stayed looking at her hand, not knowing how to handle the compliment. "I find cuts all the time and can't figure out how the heck I'm getting them." She halfway rolled her eyes, giving herself a disappointing smile.

"Well, it seems I'm always cutting myself too. Why do you think I keep band aids with me all the time? And I have to tell you that your skin is far from horrible. I think it's very lovely." Tom still had a hand on top of Joan's and ran his thumb across the back of it lightly.

"Now this was a definite pass," Joan thought, and tried matching her eyes to his. When she was able to force herself to do so, she was surprised to see how sweet his smile was and how confident he was. It weakened her, causing her to sit straighter, displaying a false sense of security that she thought she needed to show being older. "This is a very beautiful man." Tom didn't waver; relaxed, he stared at her. Joan was almost frozen. He looked around her face adoringly, now almost petting the back of her hand, careful not to touch her wedding band. He started to lean in toward her, looking into her eyes and then at her lips. They gracious parted and inviting. Joan didn't want to say anything; he was so gorgeous, and she didn't move, but she felt she was doing something wrong yet charitable. Cautiously, Tom put his bottom lip to the side of her mouth, still open. He delicately pinched her top lip with his, then her bottom lip. Joan turned her palm into Tom's, weaving her fingers through his, cupping, and tenderly feeling, then clenched it when she started pressing her lips against his. She tasted coffee, but his breath was still fresh. Tom put his free hand around the back of her neck. His hands were large and strong. Joan couldn't pull away now, she went too far and would feel like a silly schoolgirl if she did. She let herself go and let Tom pull her into him, taking his other hand from the table and putting it on her hip. So strong and so soft, and she knew that he wanted her now. This felt wonderful. There was a slam down the hallway, someone coming out of their room. They both rocked back away from each other, looking in the direction of the noise.

Katrina appeared around the corner.

"Hey," she said looking as though she just woke up in haste, quickly washing and dressing, with a pillow crease still visible along her cheek. She was preoccupied and, in a hurry, to go out the exit. She stepped back and craned her neck so she could see the clock on the wall.

"Oh boy, I can't believe I slept in. Now I'm missing most of the class," she said, disappointed in herself before going out the door. Tom and Joan watched her for a moment through the windows for some sort of assurance. They looked at each other, Tom giving a small chuckle and Joan smiling at him. He scooted his chair a little closer to her.

"Ahh. maybe we ought to hold off right now." Joan held her hand up in lame protest. Tom was wanting to touch her but instead squeezed his hands together.

"Yeah, you're right." Tom thought a minute. He thought about asking her to his room, but that seemed crude and juvenile. "Would you go out to dinner with me tonight?"

"What, and miss the play," Joan teased. "Of course, I would."

"There's this Irish restaurant and pub that I think you'd like."

"Sounds nice."

They both grinned and Joan took a deep breath, stood up, glanced around quickly, then bent over giving Tom another kiss. He wanted to pull her into him again, but she pulled away to quickly, smiled and walked out of the dorm, holding her shoulders a little squarer, knowing that he was watching her.

"So, then you can have an omniscient first-person narrator? For instance, a ghost tells a story with access to everyone's thoughts as well as their actions, right?"

"Yes, yes Mr. Hess you are right." In returning to the room Denise looked deflated and biting her bottom lip with a little uncertainty before answering any questions. A remarkable transition from the motivational speaker at the start of the class. "But seldom are stories going to be told in that perspective. And that is probably the only instance."

"Well, a story could also be told by someone with extrasensory perception."

"Yeah, but in that case, I believe it'd still be considered a first-person narrative, with the teller only having more access to other details. And not having information outside their immediate area, they wouldn't really fall under the classification of the omniscient narrative." Denise looked as though she had just scored a point, and Warren remained unaffected, knowing that his victory was not in winning the argument but in drawing Denise into it.

"Well, unless they had a peripheral." Warren was cut off.

"We can probably finish this discussion at another time, but right now I have twenty minutes left to make some points on a few other topics, so if I could, I'd like to cover those first."

"Oh sure, I didn't mean to interrupt. Please go ahead." Denise didn't know Warren, but she suspected his demeanor was insincere. She filled the rest of the class without the creative zest she had in the beginning. She was now making eye contact with everyone, but as soon as she looked at them, they looked away or down. There were no more pens or pencils moving to take notes, and there was more interest in the clock on the wall than anything else. She was even looking at it at the time. When class was over, everyone left without making any comment. Warren walked by her casually.

"If he was sincere, he'll stop and continue the conversation," Denise thought. Warren only looked at her blankly and when she tried on a courteous smile, he showed no notice of it. For the first time since high school the edge of her mouth quivered. "Look at how unkept he is. He looks like trailer trash. I'd like to put him in the company of my friends and see how uneasy he'd feel. I bet he wouldn't act so smug then."

Other than Denise, May was the only one still in the class, sitting in the back and looking down at some papers she had on her lap. To put them on the table seemed too high because she was small and slouched a great deal from osteoporosis. She kept her purse and old leather briefcase on the floor by her chair, as it was easier to pick them up than to reach up and lift them.

"You going to lunch, May?" May looked surprised, oblivious and focused on her papers. Staring through her coke bottle glasses, Denise thought she appeared funny, but sweet. And when she smiled, she looked even funnier.

"Oh, in a little bit dear, when my legs say it's okay to get up and walk again." Denise stayed in the classroom as well, looking over one of the manuscripts from one of the writers in her group. And occasionally she looked up at May, waiting until she was ready to go so, she could walk her back to the dorm.

Bobbie couldn't contain herself. Pride forced her to finally tell some of the other members that her granddaughter was going to be performing the part of Rebecca Gibbs in the Thornton Wilder play, which was the reason she'd been rallying everyone to attend. Bobbie was even going so far as to try and find those writers with the largest vehicles or most passenger room so that they could shuttle as many as possible. Joan and Tom were doing everything possible to stay away from the wave of excitement. Neither wanted to look like a party pooper or disappoint Bobbie by telling her that they had other plans. Bobbie was the matriarch of Red Creek, and many felt that to disappoint her would be bad juju.

Grace had been asking everyone if they had seen Joey anywhere, hoping to attend the play with him and then go out alone together afterwards, but no one saw Joey since the morning classes. And Warren said he had other things he wanted to do without giving any definition. Other than those four, everyone else indicated that they were going, with an "okay", nod, thumbs up, or "sure I'd be delighted." Even the War Correspondent and Abigail hinted an interest in the evenings event, leading Oscar and Jim to believe and humor themselves on how Abigail's grandmother must have better cellular service in the afterlife or state of the art internet provider such as HOL, Heaven Online. Jeff Hermann joined in the private joking after he learned the circumstances and then proved to have a pretty quick wit after loosening up with a few beers, at least for one liner. But that was essential to his trade and given his appearance and demeanor it seemed expected.

Josslyn was able to get a seat near Oscar with Dorothy sitting in between them. However, before the play started and the auditorium was still filling up, Dorothy wanted to make sure she went to the toilet, so she didn't have to fight the crowd during intermission. Oscar moved over to her empty seat, telling Josslyn that he was glad she made it.

"I didn't see you with any of the other carpools and thought maybe you decided not to come."

"No, I missed my bus, unfortunately, so I had to drive myself. But I guess it was a good thing I was late because one of the other girls missed her ride as well.

I don't think she's going to want to ride back with me though. I accidently ran a red light, and she just freaked." Josslyn accentuated the last three words, grinned, and raised her eyebrows. Oscar could only smile back at her, and he glad to see that she looked a lot more relaxed than earlier.

"Well, if you were running late, you should've just let one of us know. I'm sure any one of groups riding together would've been more than happy to wait for you."

"I would've but I got hung up for a little bit and I wasn't in a position to get a hold of anyone."

"Oh, were you on the phone with someone?" Oscar hoped his subtle question would answer another question, "Were you talking to your boyfriend?"

"No, I was actually hung up. Like an idiot I locked my keys in my room, but I knew that I left my window partially opened. And being on the ground floor, I didn't think that I'd have any problem just pushing it all the way open and then shimmying through it. But those darn windows don't open as wide as I thought. Not only that, but they're like three feet off the ground. So, by the time you get half of your body through, you don't have any kind of leverage with either your feet or your arms." Oscar was picturing the image of Josslyn stuck with her body teetering, trying in vain to touch the floor of the room with her hands or her toes trying to reach the ground outside. He had a smile that was ready to burst into laughter at any moment, plus her serious manner made the story funnier as she raised her brows in astonishment and demonstrated movement with her hands. "Finally, I was able to get my hips through, but my belt loop got caught. I couldn't back out to release myself without ripping my pants, so I had to keep one hand on the floor and with the other I could unzip my pants and slide through the window, but then they twisted around my ankles like my feet were shackled together." Josslyn barely glanced at Oscar and thought he was getting bored with her story. "Anyway, I eventually worked my feet free and so here I am."

"Well, I'm glad you were able to make it." Oscar felt such a delight for Josslyn at that moment that a simple smile replaced his laugh. Josslyn felt extremely comfortable, but she would've been around anyone at that time. The part of the story that she left out was the pain she felt when her coffee burns earlier that morning were pressed against the window edges. After running to the bathroom to rub more ointment and crying for a time, she popped four Ultracets at once to help relieve the stinging and throbbing. But knowing that those would take a while to affect her, she also took a couple shots of ginger brandy that she brought to the conference with her. The calm and numbness she felt started shortly before she ran the red light, allowing her to take her passengers screams so flippantly.

Elaine had hoped that Warren would've come along, because they always had so much to talk about when they were together. They were part of the same generation and started out in life with the same ideas and wrestled many of the same demons. Her husband was the only other person that she felt that connection with. However tonight, Elaine found herself sitting with Noah, Katrina, and Barnell. Barnell was restless, rocking back and forth in the spring cushioned seats. It wasn't rapidly like a child, but it wasn't at the pace of Whistler's Mother either. That was his nature though, fueled by nervous energy. Noah was seventy-seven and although he was a businessman most of his adult life, increasingly he became intolerable of people, turning into a grumpy old man. The quiet, slow, and methodical rhythm of retirement was making him impatient. He knew the format of the play. The college was doing it in its original direction when it came out in 1938, where the stage manager with a hat and pipe (though in his early twenties) pulls chairs and tables out from behind the curtains and arranges them stage left and right while the audience continues to take their seats. When everyone is seated and the props are in place, the house lights are dimmed, and then the stage manager begins his monologue. But no one seemed anxious to take their seats; they were socializing, posturing, and talking on their cell phones. Noah remembered the days when people were much more courteous, taking their seats as soon as possible with anticipation and some level of respect for others around them.

Noah watched the poor young man on the stage trying to look as though he was still busy, although the tables, chairs, and bench were already in place. The crowd was stalling the momentum, and Noah had used up all his conversation for polite society with Barnell. He would've preferred sitting between Elaine and Katrina or at least beside one of the two ladies, but instead he got stuck on the end with this autistic rocking child next to him, which Noah was old enough to be a grandfather to.

"Excuse me, but do you really need to do all that rocking?" Barnell looked at Noah, surprised, while in the middle of biting one of his nails. He spit the piece of nail toward the floor.

"Sorry," Barnell said, not wanting to offend Noah and as though he were used to people correcting his behavior. Less than a minute later, Barnell was bouncing his knee up and down. Noah caught it out of the corner of his eye and tried to ignore it, but it was becoming like a magnet, stronger and stronger with each passing second. He remembered why he liked "Our Town" at the age of sixteen, but it wasn't the same reason now. Really, he wasn't sure if he'd like it at all, even if the performances were impeccable. Just before the bombing of Pearl Harbor, his mother took him to an off off broadway production of the play. It was grand and the most memorable experience of his life prior to the war. The characters among the dead, sitting in their chairs as the ghosts in the cemetery, talking about the living and departed, was comforting to Noah. It was an idea that he took with himself when he joined the fight in Europe in 1943. It was soothing to him to believe, that if killed in battle, he'd return home to the people he loved. To be reunited with others that died and watch those still living. But now he felt uncomfortably close to death, seeing his wife pass away two years prior. He felt uncertain and aggravated. Other relatives, people that he worked with, buddies during the war, all seemed too much to fill a cemetery adequately.

The steady sound of voices was turning into a hum. People kept brushing against his arm from the aisle, which he couldn't understand because it seemed plenty wide enough. And Barnell's leg seemed to be picking up speed. The stage manager was beginning to look ridiculous, adjusting and readjusting the props on stage while waiting for the crowd to settle. Noah thought, "Why in the hell doesn't this kid just go backstage and sit it out for a while?" then stood up in frustration and walked back toward the lobby. Barnell looked after him, still chewing on his nails.

And Elaine and Katrina seemed too involved in their conversation to notice that Noah had left. He met Dorothy and Jim by the restrooms and complained about the lack of enthusiasm or total disregard for immediate seating.

Bobbie did the best she could ahead of time to ensure seats for group members but could only get three or four chairs together at a time, spaced randomly throughout the auditorium. Bobbie took Grace, Julie, and Jack Bulfinch (a returning writer who knew Bobbie well but missed the last three conferences) with her to set up in the best seats, in the center column, the fourth row from the stage. There were balconies, but all the writers' received tickets for the main floor. The auditorium seemed new or fairly modern looking in design, which took away from the feel of being at the theater and gave more the impression of attending an award ceremony or expecting a celebrity speaker to talk about their new book.

Jeff Hermann and another Jeff, about the same age (and who has been coming to the conference for three years now), were seated together, along with May between them. Bobbie gave them the next best seats, knowing that May needed to be close to appreciate the play and relatively close to the exit as well. Everyone else she let pair up haphazardly, and they did, all just grabbing a ticket without checking the assignment.

In the lobby, Jim was telling a story about himself and a group of friends, largely Jewish, during college and prior to law school when they went to see "Bent" by Martin Sherman at the Apollo Theater in 1979. Dorothy was impressed that Jim went to the Apollo but had never heard of "Bent" and wondered why he emphasized his friend's beliefs.

"So, what does being Jewish have to do with whether they liked the play or not?"

"Well, the play is about Hitler's persecution and imprisonment of homosexuals in Berlin leading up to the war. Before the play, little, if any, knew or talked about that aspect of the Holocaust."

"Oh, I see." Dorothy rocked her head back. Noah only raised his brows for a second. He was preoccupied and really paid little attention to Jim's story. He gave an ambiguous response only because he caught Jim and Dorothy looking at him at the same time. A younger man was standing behind him, talking on a cell phone. He would occasionally step from one side to the other or stand and sway, brushing against Noah. It was fairly packed in the lobby, but Noah couldn't imagine someone being so ignorant that they couldn't feel themselves rubbing against someone.

"Yeah, and you could picture the sentiment in 79'. It didn't quite receive the fanfare that the critics claimed it did. What pulled it off however was putting Richard Gere in the lead role."

For a moment, Noah thought the young guy had left because he didn't hear him talking, or rather chuckling, over the phone, nor did he feel the brushing. Then came another good brush. Noah was pissed. He shoved his elbow into the young man's back.

"Ahhh," the man shouted. Noah turned around and found, not the young fast tracker, but an old man, seemingly older than he, now with one hand on the area Noah jabbed his elbow into and the other steadying himself on an aluminum cane.

"I'm terribly sorry."

"What the hell is your problem, mister?" The old man was still rubbing his back and stepped toward Noah. He had on a suit and tie that seemed more appropriate for a funeral. Jim and Dorothy didn't notice the jab and were confused by the confrontation. When the man shouted from the pain, it drew the attention of several other people that were nearby, including the younger man on the cell phone.

"I am very sorry. I thought you were someone else." But Noah couldn't give his apology with much conviction; though shocked that he elbowed an innocent bystander, he was still relatively pissed. The old man sensed the insincerity in his voice and wacked Noah just above his knee with his cane.

"Oww…you son-of-a-bitch."

"Oh, I'm sorry. I thought you were someone else." Noah lunged toward the old man. Dorothy was close and quick enough to wrap her arms around Noah, but she lost leverage in her high heels and only added weight to the attack, causing the three to fall into the young man with the cell phone and an usher, which knocked them both backward down a short flight of carpeted steps leading to the exit. Dorothy, Noah, and the old man ended up filleted at the top of the steps, immediately sitting, or raising up on one arm to see if the two young men were alright. The usher, a college student, seemingly athletic-looking with gel in his hair, was blatantly more embarrassed than hurt. His face was reddened by the awkward tumble and landing in a straddled position on the back of the other man, who was lying face down. Frantically, he jumped to his feet, less concerned about the man's well-being underneath him than about being seen in that situation.

"Are you okay sir?" the usher asked the man that was on the cell phone after he collected himself.

"Ah, yeah," he replied with a slow uncertainty and a groan.

"Here, lemme help you up." While the usher was helping the other young man on the landing, Dorothy helped Noah, and Jim helped the old man, with a couple bystanders giving meager assistance. Those in the crowd that had seen most of it unfold were whispering to each other and fighting laughter, while the rest were just curious. Two other ushers and a middle-aged woman who seemed to be an authority figure at the theater pushed their way through the lobby crowd.

"Okay, what happened?" The woman directed her question more toward the usher on the landing at the bottom of the steps than anyone else. Having helped the other man to his feet, the usher pointed to the top of the steps, but before he could say anything else, another young college student stepped forward, again with gelled hair, short, cropped clothes, and earrings, but a heavier set.

"Those two elderly gentlemen got into a fight and knocked those other guys down the stairs." The man with the cane raised it in the air as though he was going to hit the witness, but one of the other ushers caught his arm before he could do anything.

"I'll show you 'elderly' you pimply faced bastard."

There were a few "hey's" and "whoa's", Noah gave the college student a disgusted stare.

"Tattle tale."

"Is everyone alright?" The woman was obviously more concerned about Noah and the man with the cane, particularly him, than she was the two at the bottom of the stairs. The cell phone guy was the only one to answer, but no one paid attention.

"Okay, well I'm going to have to ask you two gentlemen to leave. And if there is a problem, I'll just have to call campus security and have you escorted."

"Let go of me," the old man said jerking himself from Jim and the usher, then adjusting his suit. Jim looked over at Noah.

"You want me to give you a ride back, Noah?" Jim brought several people with him to the theater, though his car was small.

"No, no that's alright. I don't want you guys to miss your show."

"Really, Noah, I don't mind." Dorothy added a look of "please let Jim drive you back".

"I said it's alright. I'll take a cab. It's no big deal." The sound of Noah's voice was too exact now. To make any more offers, it was easy to tell, would try Noah's patience.

"Sir, do you have someone here that you want to get a hold of?" the woman asked the other man in a tone that a person would use when trying to help a child.

"Get away from me," the old man said bitterly. "I walked to this goddamn place by myself, and I'll walk home by myself." There were a few snickers in the crowd, and so the old man waved his cane back and forth in front of him to clear a path toward the exit, not intending to hit anyone, but keeping everyone on their toes.

Dorothy and Jim walked Noah toward the other exit at the opposite end of the lobby with two of the ushers behind them for insurance, while the woman talked with the man who had the cell phone, perhaps to avoid any legal repercussions.

Jim was about to insist on taking Noah back to campus but thought better of himself. And he really wouldn't have minded. He rode over with Liz, Beverly, Denise and a second-year attendee named Brandon Hare a dowdy looking but outspoken Baptist who wrote periodicals for religious publications and was working on a novel length story similar to the prodigal son. Liz and Beverly were attempting to be racy in front of Denise in the hopes to impress her, but Brandon put a black cloud over their uninhibited foray, by bringing in the "teachings of Christ". An argument almost erupted when Jim pulled into the theater parking lot and raised his voice above the others and said, "We're here." Jim was just thankful he didn't have Abigail in his car.

"Are you okay, young lady?" Noah asked Dorothy just before he was about to step through the door and working a concerned smile. Dorothy appreciated it.

"Yeah, of course I am. I take a hell of a lot harder tumbles than that every week…only not in high heels." Jim let out a little chuckle. Dorothy leaned over and kissed Noah on the cheek. "You take it easy going back to the dorm."

"Oh, don't you worry about me." Noah then shook Jim's hand.

"Catch ya tonight after the old timer." Noah then left. Jim thought he shouldn't have said "old timer", but Noah didn't look offended.

Out on the sidewalk in front of the building Noah saw the old man with the cane standing under one of the lamp posts in the parking lot, rubbing his hip. Seeing him wasn't a surprise to Noah, he turned in that direction on purpose, but noticing how sore he looked was a surprise, sort of. He walked over toward him. Within thirty feet the old man heard Noah's hard soled dress shoes. He looked over his shoulder gradually and turned away with the same calm. Noah slowed his steps which were already apprehensive.

"Did ya come ta try and finish what ya started?" The old man kept his back to him as he spoke.

"No. I came to apologize."

"Ahh" Noah paused.

"Is your hip alright?"

"Yeah, it's fine. It's just this goddamn plate they put in after the war. It's given me trouble ever since."

"The Pacific or Europe?"

"Pacific. You?"

"Europe."

"What year dija go in?"

"Forty-three."

"Forty-two myself." Noah thought the old man was in as soon as the war started or enlisted in the armed services prior to that. Noah considered himself much younger, but he wasn't. He was probably only a year younger.

"Can I buy you a drink?" The man looked at his watch through the bifocal part of his glasses, holding his arm up for the light and his head back so he could read it.

"Well, it's not past my bedtime yet. I don't see the harm. If you don't mind the walk-about a block and a half-there's an old Irish pub that serves good cheap scotch."

"Sounds like my kinda bar." They walked through the parking lot, toward the street, as if they were walking in their own yards, Noah occasionally bending a little to rub his leg.

"I think we should've been dead years ago."

"Yeah, we should've."

The play had started just as Dorothy and Jim got back to their seats. Dorothy noticed Josslyn was more talkative than normal, even well into the first act. If she hadn't liked her so much, she would've found her annoying. By the second act, Josslyn was much more docile, slumping down in her seat and leaning on the armrest next to Oscar. For a short time in the third act, Josslyn was sitting up again but nodding off, sometimes catching herself with a jolt of her body, causing her chair to rock. When the actor playing Constable Warren said good morning to Mr. Webb and then added, "You're up early," Josslyn was so deep in sleep that she let out a loud snore. The audience laughed. The actor on stage who was playing Mr. Webb, hearing the snore, ad-libbed, "obviously before the critics." The audience laughed again, at which point both Oscar, Dorothy, and Abigail, who had been sitting in the row behind them, all nudged Josslyn awake.

The play ended with a standing ovation, due in one part to the ad-lib, another part that it was a college play and a lot of parents and other relatives attended, and another part that all the actors delivered their lines effortlessly. Plus, people give standing ovations very easily anymore. If enough people stand, then most of the rest feel guilty and follow suit regardless of what they really thought of the performance.

Oscar drove Josslyn's car back to the dorm. Not because of his own concern but because Dorothy insisted he do it as well. Josslyn didn't put up any argument and was actually happy that he asked to drive, knowing that she'd be able to spend a little more time alone with him. However, the sleep in the theater didn't seem like enough for her, and when she got back into the comfort of her own car, plus the comfort she felt near Oscar, she became lethargic again. It was as though the pills were time-released and the bulk of their effect, including the alcohol mix, was too much to fight. When they got back to the dorm, Josslyn was sound asleep again.

"Josslyn. Josslyn. Come on, honey, it's time to get up." Oscar caught himself that time calling her honey. He was surprised that it came out so easily. He knew he could pick her up and carry her to the dorm without challenge, but somehow it seemed inappropriate now that he realized how attracted he was to her. Handling patients of all shapes, sizes, and genders was never much of a concern to him, and he always did so without hardly a second thought. But now he couldn't. Seeing her lie there with her head arched back against the window and showing her beautiful neck, he was afraid he'd want to just hold her in his arms, caress her, and bury his face in her hair.

"Huh? what? are we here?"

"Yup, we're here." Oscar got out of the car went around to Josslyn's door to help her out, but she sat up quickly, refreshed in the short drive back to the Welty campus, and was ready to get out of the car on her own. However, she waited and watched Oscar take long strides in his almond-colored khaki pants around the front of the car. He wore a light blue button-down shirt under a black dress coat. She didn't tell him how nice he looked, but she decided before they got to the dorm that she would. Oscar opened the door, standing with it between them, holding one arm up for direction, and slightly bowing.

"Most gracious and kind lady, I offer full bend and tender travel to thy lair." Josslyn smiled, blushed, and stood up in front of Oscar on the other side of the door.

"Hamlet? Othello?"

"Neither. I just made it up," Oscar said with a grin and straightening up.

"I'm impressed." Josslyn looked down at the ground, wanting to somehow work in telling Oscar that he looked nice. "Thanks for driving back." Josslyn tried looking up into Oscar's eyes, but it was hard; they were standing too close together.

"Oh, I'm glad I did." Josslyn stepped away from the arch of the door to shut it but paused. She created a little distance and was able to look up.

"You look really nice tonight." Oscar shifted on one foot, took his hand off the door, and rested it on the edge of the roof.

"Well, thanks. And you look splendid." Oscar turned his head upon hearing the door slam on the main dorm. Josslyn became nervous, looked away, and, not noticing where Oscar rested his hand, shut the car door on his thumb.

"Ahhh…Shit!…Oh God, that hurts!"

Noah was milking his second scotch. The man with the cane enjoyed the drink, and now on his third, he didn't appear to be losing his momentum, but he had already told Noah about helping his pappy as a boy run a moonshine still. The bar was a lot nicer than Noah expected, being attached to one of those generic restaurants that serve pretty much the same as any other place, like Friday's, or Ruby Tuesday's, or Ponderosa. Four-foot-high partitions were the only thing separating those on a liquid diet from those on a solid food diet. And like the other restaurants, it had its own theme, and that being Irish, though hokey, it still gave it a unique atmosphere with old, regenerated photographs of Irish boxers from the early 1900's and late 1800's. Its menu had ethnic names like O'Grady's Grill Cheese and Sullivan's Sirloin. The corned beef and cabbage plate with the Feast or Famine Baked Potato was seldom ordered but remained at the top of the menu for novelty purposes. There were ceramic leprechauns sitting in various locations around the dining area. Some stood poised behind plants as if hiding. A two- foot-by-two-foot autographed picture of the Irish Rovers hung on the wall near the entrance, and in the middle of the restaurant, where the ceiling vaulted at its highest point, an Irish flag was suspended.

"Writing huh? That's what brought you here?"

"Mostly, yeah."

"Ever git anythin published?" Noah didn't want to tell him that he had his memoirs published from his World War Two experiences. That usually brought criticism or testiness from other veterans, but he couldn't lie, not to this man, but he thought he might be able to slog through telling him whole truth.

"Yeah, years ago." Noah took a hard sallow. "What kinda book was it?"

"Ahh…nonfiction, character driven. A sort of coming-of-age story." The other man laughed.

"So ya wrote about your war experiences." Saying as a statement the man looked over the top of his glasses at Noah.

"Well." Noah wanted to explain his reasons for doing it, but the chance to bullshit was senseless. "Yeah…yeah. I guess I thought I had something to say back then. I thought somebody wanted to hear what I had to say."

"I take it the book didn't do very well?"

"Nope. I ended up buying back the rest of the copies and giving them away to relatives." Noah and the other man laughed.

"I hope you made us all look like heroes."

"Well, I made myself look like one anyway." They both laughed again. Noah took another drink, lifting his head back and glancing in the mirror behind the bar. In it, he saw Joan standing up from one of the booths behind him. He turned to get a better look at her. She was talking to someone sitting in her booth, but Noah couldn't see who it was. Her demeanor made it look as though it was her husband. Plus, the beautiful dress she had on, along with a little more makeup, suggested to Noah that they were spending a night on the town. It looked as though she was going to the restroom which was near the bar. Noah thought he'd surprise her.

"Excuse me for a minute," Noah told his drinking buddy. He walked in line with one of the beams, so Joan couldn't see his face as she walked toward him. She had to come on his side of the beam in order to get to the toilet. Noah stepped in front of her.

"Hi"

"Ah. Oh, Noah." Joan's eyes widened.

"What are you doing here, dear? A night on the town with your husband?" Joan wondered for a moment if Noah was speaking sarcastically and saw her with Tom or was serious and didn't see them together. But Noah didn't seem the type to try and make an uncomfortable situation worse. So many things raced through her head, but nothing seemed plausible. Noah was probably the worst person from the writer's group for her to meet, because he always seemed very noble and more honest to her than most anyone she'd ever met.

"No, I'm just here with a friend." Noah's eyes slightly squinted indicating a hint of suspicion. Joan had to try and mislead him. "And what are you doing here?"

"Just having a drink with a friend, myself." Noah glanced over Joan's shoulder. Tom was standing up next to the booth, taking his jacket off and hanging on the rack next to his seat. He glanced at Noah talking to Joan and Noah matched his eyes. Tom knew it was too late to duck back into the booth, so he gave a quick wave and then sat down. Noah tried to nod just enough that Tom would recognize the greeting but not draw attention from Joan who was looking around room as she started asking how the play went. But she still caught the nod and seeing the direction of it, was certain who it was for. However, she pretended not to notice.

"Well...actually I didn't get to see the play. Another gentleman and I were kicked out for fighting in the lobby." Noah smiled like Stan Laurel, someone he liked to imitate when he was much younger and looked a lot like. He mentioned the incident knowing it would be a distraction from an otherwise awkward moment.

"Oh, my goodness." Joan looked shocked and put her hand on Noah's arm. "Are you okay?" Noah was hoping that Joan would see the humor in it, but at the same time knew better.

"Yes, of course. There really wasn't much of a struggle. Dorothy saw to that." Tom walked up behind Joan after realizing how pathetic it may have looked if he didn't at least come over and say hi to Noah.

"Hey, how you doin' Noah," Tom said strained, but hiding it well, or well enough. Joan was beside herself. She thought how she hadn't felt this foolish since she was sixteen and her mother caught her and a boy necking in their garage.

"I'm doing good, Tom. And yourself?" If not for Joan's embarrassment, Noah felt he could be enjoying it.

"Fine." They shook hands. "Would you like to join us for dinner," Tom offered, with the polite sense that Noah would turn him down.

"Oh, no thanks, I couldn't."

"Yeah, that sounds like a good idea," Joan encouraged, and Tom wished she hadn't, but no evidence appeared on his face.

"Oh, no, really, I."

"Please Noah, I insist." Joan was feeling much more comfortable in pressuring Noah, and Tom couldn't believe her disregard for him or their situation, but his good manners still made it look as though he was just as enthusiastic as Joan… well almost. His eyes became a little more fixed and his grin a little more like a clinch of his teeth. "And invite your friend." Tom wanted to gulp. He didn't know about the friend.

"Alright, but you have to let me pay for the meal."

"Fantastic," Joan said, putting her hand back on Noah's arm as if that bonded the agreement.

"Great." Tom felt as though his face had frozen into that would be impossible to thaw.

They all made it to their rented beds that evening or, like Oscar, in the early morning hours of the following day, after having his thumb reset and splinted at a nearby clinic. He's had worse accidents and didn't mind the broken thumb. Letting Josslyn hold his hand and stay with him until they returned to their rooms was worth it to Oscar. Even the throbbing discomfort that occasionally woke him in the night allowed him to recap their evening together and using his writer's imagination to create more romantic scenes. Other attendees slept uneasily that night, and some hardly at all. A few slept better than they had in days or years after masturbating like Tom or from the excitement, alcohol, and a good meal like Noah. There were those that had a regimen of sleep and were unaffected by environment or circumstance, like Julie. When it came time to sleep, she could tune out any troubles from the day and drift into her six hours of routine slumber. Then there was Warren, who stayed up the whole night reading a manuscript. But the rest slept or stared at the ceiling alone, including Grace, consoled only by their imaginations in either dreams or conscientiousness, scrutinized by some spirit, God of choosing, or some mythological creature. Only a very few found tangible companionship.

Jim burst through his door the following morning after being woken by a noise and thinking that he was about to discover the mystery of who was making the coffee, but to his disappointment and as near as he could tell, someone had placed an empty, tall, narrow trash can by the window, and a heavy gust of wind coming from the south had blown it over. It was still rocking back and forth on its side when Jim stepped into the lobby. He turned his attention toward the coffee table and noticed the pots were already made.

"Shit. I missed it again." He went back to his room and put on his pink slippers. Jim returned just as Grace came out of her room.

"What was that noise?"

"I think the wind knocked over the trash can." There was a stack of paper towels on top of the fridge by the open window. Another gust came through, this time blowing the stack like confetti around one end of the room. Jim ran over and shut the window before there was a chance of something else being knocked over or blown around. Grace and Jim started picking up the napkins. Grace looked out the window and watched the trees beyond the courtyard on the open ground. The plumes of the hardwood trees (maple, oak, and apple) were flopping through the air like a cheerleader's pom poms, Grace thought.

"Jesus, look at that wind." Jim stopped for a moment without a great deal of concern.

"It looks like we've got a storm coming through." They finished picking up the napkins, and Jim turned on the television. The local news was still on minutes before being passed on to the major network, but they were cutting to commercials, saying they'd return with the doppler radar weather forecast. Warren walked in from outside, with his hair tousled by the wind. He combed it down with his fingers.

"Y'all are up early." Warren walked over to Grace on his way to the coffee pot. Grace was sitting in a chair with her feet on the seat and her legs folded up against her; she had sat that way in the mornings since she was a kid. Warren squeezed her shoulder. "Hey sexy, plan on giving everyone a hard time with those silk pajamas this morning?" Grace smiled and patted his hand before he let go.

"A girl's got to aim high if she wants to get

ahead." Grace smiled because of her loaded answer, anticipating Warren's response.

"It sounds like you're aiming below the belt to me, but I don't think you've ever set your sights any higher." Jim looked at Grace to see if she took the last comment as a jab, but he was used to their dialogue and seldom participated, often turning his attention elsewhere only out of boredom. A small part of him had contempt for Grace and women like her who took their beauty for granted. Then another part of him admired her. And yet another part of him didn't find her beautiful at all, most times. But this morning, those lavender silk pajamas, smoothly draped over the mounds and curves of her body would draw the even attention of a castrato.

A young married couple that was attending the conference for the first time, came in from outside. They were urban professionals with no children and a lifetime membership at their local spa and country club. They tried adopting a foreign child and failing, primarily because they just gave up, decided to collaborate on a book explaining their trials and tribulations in fighting through all the red tape. To someone's benefit, them not being able to adopt was the better part of the system at work. Moved by the Sally Struthers commercials, they thought the adoption would be a win win situation all around: they would be doing charitable work, have a child without the inconvenience of pregnancy, and have a poor foreign kid to show off to their friends and family.

"Whew, boy, that wind is something else." The man was loud and usually laughed along with everything he said. He was sculpted and had a black belt in Tai Kwan Do. His wife was certain to join in the chorus of laughter with him. Jim, Warren, and Grace could only stare at them. It was still too early in the morning to be extroverted and talk loudly.

"I sure am glad I didn't have my hair done today," said the lady, looking at Grace and chuckling as though she had found a kindred spirit. Grace only raised her eyebrows. The lady was attractive, with a very athletic body. She was wearing her blonde hair in a tight bun, but even when she dressed up for dinner and other occasions, there was something about her being too clean, too energetic, too outgoing, and too upbeat that ruined any of her sex appeal. She had no sensuality about her. However, Grace didn't notice this and thought she was the type, if any, that guys would pick over her: educated, physically fit, obviously from a good upbringing, and always presentable. Grace believed she would be the perfect girl to take home to Mom. "I love your pajamas. Where'd you get them, Marshall Fields?"

"No, Neiman Marcus." Grace was surprised to see the lady nod as though she took her answer seriously, even with the seasoning of sarcasm. Grace didn't know where the hell the pajamas came from. They were a gift from Joey, whom she was hoping to see this morning, knowing that the pajamas would turn him on. There was no way she could've afforded these pajamas. She lived and raised her two daughters in a trailer. And that she didn't even own but rented, fucking the landlord to get out of paying the security deposit. When he approached her later, saying that they could work something out for a bounced check, she threatened to tell his wife, and that she'd have the money to him the next day, which she did after fucking an ex-boyfriend.

Jim found the tension that Grace created amusing, whereas Warren didn't notice being instructed on the finer points of coffee cuisine after asking the husband if he wanted a cup. Jim also noticed the strange and extra-long pause that the woman was giving Grace.

"So, what do you write?" the woman asked looking Grace up and down, giving no notice to Jim.

"Romance, erotica."

"Fiction, I imagine."

Jim couldn't see this conversation having a happy ending and with the hand he had in his lap, was keeping his fingers crossed that it wouldn't.

"Yes, of course. I'm afraid it'd be too racy if I wrote based on personal experiences. But then again, I thought I could turn it into a training guide for young couples trying to have children." Grace shrugged her shoulders with a mocking grin. Undeniably, Grace's comment was enough of a blow to weaken the other woman's offenses. She said nothing, kept the smile she came to the table with and walked over to her husband who was still talking to Warren without his attention, explaining with great enthusiasm about a coffee shop slash bookstore he went to in Seattle Washington. She placed her hand in the middle of her husband's back. This must've been a signal they've worked out together on other occasions, as he leaned to her with his ear, she whispered something, he excused himself to Warren and they both left.

"Wow. That was weird." Grace stared at Jim. "Can you believe that lady?"

"That was pretty odd."

"Yeah, and thanks for all your help." Jim had to bite his lip before answering. "Well, you looked as though you were doing pretty well on your own. Besides, you started it."

"I started it? Whose side you on? That chick was being smug, and you know it. Just because she has nice, perky breasts, you think she's little miss innocent."

"What? You're being ridiculous." Warren sat down at the table. "What's this all about?"

"Oh, Anna Nicole Smith over here feels threatened by the aerobics instructor that just passed through."

"Fuck you, Jim." With that, Grace left the table and went back to her room. "I take it Grace hasn't gotten a hold of Joey yet," Jim asked Warren. "Apparently not."

"Well, maybe she'll see him today. He's scheduled for a morning class." There was a flash of lightning outside. Jim and Warren turned their heads and looked out at the sky, waiting for the sound of the thunder, Jim whispering the seconds to himself until he heard it.

"One one thousand, two one thousand, three one thousand, and four one thousand." Then Warren farted, before the sound of thunder. Jim shot him a disgusting look.

"It sounds like the storm's getting awfully close." Warren grinned.

"Oh, God." Jim put his hand over his mouth and nose, stood from the table and walked over to the window.

"I heard that the storm's s'pose to pass by noon, and then it's gonna clear up."

"Probably before that smell goes away. What did you eat?"

Denise Domikowski walked through the door on the other side of the room escorting May on her arm.

"Here ya go hon," Denise said letting May step over the threshold, keeping the door open with her body, and shaking the umbrella outside.

"Thank you dear." Warren shouted to May from across the room.

"The usual May?" Warren got up and poured some coffee in a black ceramic cup that was hidden behind the microwave, added two packets of sugar, stirred it, and sat it down at the table just as May sat down with Jim holding her arm.

"Oh, will you look at this, I've got all kinds of people helping me this morning."

"How ya feeling this morning, May?" Warren asked, putting his hand on her forearm after he sat back down.

"Actually, the arthritis isn't as bad this morning considering the weather."

"I'll catch you in class, May. I've got some material I have to go over." Denise walked to the door and not without giving Warren a distasteful glance.

"Okay dear." Denise left the room. "I think that tea Abigail gave me last night really helped." Jim looked at May curious.

"You don't believe that hocus pocus do you May?"

"At my age honey, you believe in anything and everything. Why do think us old people get taken advantage of so often. Besides, if we weren't so gullible, you'd probably never get a jury to sympathize with any of your cases." Warren laughed in light huffs of breath.

"What class you going to this morning, May,"

Warren asked. "I'm thinking about Buzz Synder's class, Chapter to Chapter."

"What's that about?"

"From what I gather, it's about how to create conflict, tension, or suspense at the end of each chapter in order make the reader want to quickly go on to the next."

"Sounds like cheap sensationalism to me," Jim interrupted. Besides, it's not like the guy writes mystery. He writes erotica for Christ sakes." May shrugged and gave a sympathetic nod. "How many people break from chapter to chapter when they're reading anyway? Isn't that what bookmarks are for? And most books don't even need chapters. I think they're seriously overdone and antiquated."

"Is your manuscript separated by chapters?" May asked hoping to end Jim's tirade.

"Well, yeah but…that's only because one of those editors I spoke with last year suggested I do it."

There was another lightening flash outside and in two seconds a thunderclap.

Abigail burst through the door nearest the table. She looked frantic.

Abigail was breathing heavily. "There's a rat in my room."

"A rat! Come on, Abigail, these dorms are old, but I don't think they're infested with rats," Jim complained, certain that she was directing her comments at him, although her other eye was fixed on Warren. "Well, it's a lot bigger than a mouse and smaller than a cat."

"Where'd you see it?" Warren asked.

"It ran along the wall under the register, then under the other bed." Warren was surprised by Abigail's panic. She never seemed threatened by the physical world. Nor the type that would be squeamish around rats, snakes, bats, or anything that could be tossed in a cauldron to make a potion. "I think the spirit is trying to keep me from the seance tonight." That explained it to Warren.

"Come on. I'll go with you, and we'll have a

look." Warren directed Abigail out of the lobby and back toward her dorm.

"Great. That's all we need, to have those agents get wind of rats at this conference and we'd be lucky to get a one of them to show up for next year's retreat," Jim said aloud, not necessarily to May.

"I wouldn't worry too much about that. Aren't all the agents from New York?"

When Abigail and Warren opened the door to her room a small hairy figure darted across the ceiling pipes, going through a small hole and into the next room. Warren ran next door and knocked. He gave the occupant no reasonable time to answer before knocking again. The door opened only a foot. Liz stood there puzzled in only a large pink tee shirt with "creative people must be stopped" written on the front in green letters that looked as though they were painted on in brush strokes. She had obviously just woken up from the knock on the door, squinting from the hallway lights.

"Excuse me, Liz." Warren was in a hurry to find out who the culprit was, and when he found out, he didn't think Liz would mind the intrusion. So, he pushed the door open farther and looked up at the ceiling. There, frozen, and ready to jump somewhere toward freedom, was a red squirrel, its tail poised like a question mark. Abigail, standing right behind Warren, pointed at the rodent.

"There's your rat, Abigail." But Abigail was looking down at the bed. Liz screamed when the squirrel jumped down on her desk and then out of the floor window that was left wide open. "And that's how it got in here." Warren shook his head. "Sorry, Liz, but we thought Abigail had a rat in her room. Oh, good morning, Beverly." Warren had just realized that Beverly was in bed.

"Morning," she replied, less polite and more nervous. Warren turned to Abigail after glancing at the other bed. It was made up and unused. He looked at Abigail.

"It looks like we solved the mystery." Warren left the room, herding Abigail at the same time. "See you gals later, and sorry again for the bother." Abigail followed Warren down the hallway and back toward the main lobby. Neither one wanted to mention what they noticed; they were being tactful, but none- the-less, they were both surprised to find out that the two housewives from Chicago were sleeping together. Warren couldn't help thinking of having a threesome with Liz and Beverly, but he only entertained the thought briefly. It wasn't that he was really attracted to either one as a separate entity, but together, two conservative housewives letting go their inhibitions, had a tremendous amount of appeal to him.

"Oh, my God. Why in the hell did you make your bed yesterday?"

"Easy Lizzie. You know I always make the beds in the morning, and you do too. How were we supposed to know Warren would be bursting into our room?"

"This is just fucking great. Now everyone here is going to know that we sleep together." Liz was pacing the floor with one hand on top of her head and the other on her hip. "Ahh!" She tilted her head back in defeat while standing by the window; though the blinds were hanging down, they were rotated so she could walk out into the parking lot. The bushes on the other side, toward the expressway, were flopping violently from the wind. Beverly came up behind Liz; she was a half a head taller. She rested her chin on Liz's shoulder and wrapped her arms around her, settling a hand on her stomach and another on her chest, just below her neck. Liz dropped both of her arms.

"Listen sweetie, we only see these people once a year. It's not like we have to see them at the PTA meetings. Besides, they're all writers. It's not like they're part of the moral majority." Liz let out a small, controlled laugh. "Also, who knows about us? A witch and a troll." They both giggled. Liz put her hands on top of Beverly's.

"And what are we?" Liz asked. "Woodland nymphs."

"Don't you mean woodland nymphos?"

Beverly kissed her neck. Liz dropped her head to the side to expose more of her neck. Beverly slid her hand down further. Liz hurried and pulled up her tee shirt, enough so Beverly could work her fingers between her legs without any interference.

Joey Goode had just introduced his session Making Time To Write to the attendees when Grace walked in.

"Morning Grace. If you want to have a seat, I haven't even started the class yet." To the trained eye on knowing for a period of time, it was evident that his attitude changed slightly in Graces presence. He was a little worried knowing her extroverted personality on what her behavior might be. He knew that she would be upset that he avoided her the last couple of days. Just as Grace walked passed him toward an aisle seat and gazed into his eyes, lightening flashed outside. Joey's eyes widened, wanting in those two seconds to say, "Heaven has no rage like love to hatred turned, nor hell a fury like a woman scorned," but censored himself by fear. Oscar, sitting next to Josslyn, was the only other attendee, knowing Joey and Grace's relationship that noticed the coincidence or made a connection.

The weather outside subsided by the time the class was over, and inside Grace made it seem like the calm before the storm before the real storm, quiet and still, following Joey around the room with her eyes, expressionless and patient. When everyone was finally gone, Joey walked over and shut the door. He knew he had to face up to Grace, and the less that could hear the better.

"Let."

"Do not start out with 'let me explain'." Grace was holding up a finger like crossing guard with their sign. "The way you are supposed to begin is 'first, let me apologize.'" But Joey was going to begin with "Let me apologize." However, he didn't want to interrupt Grace. Not at this point anyway. Knowing what he wanted to tell her, he thought it would be a good idea to let her have some control and blow off a little steam.

"Okay, first let me apologize."

"Great. Now you say, 'I have been a real jerk, and I should've called, or left a message, or something." Grace stood up and walked toward Joey.

"I've been a real jerk, and I should've called, or left a message, or something."

"Very good, Mr. Goode. You seem to be a quick study. Now you say, 'however, tonight I'd like to take you out for dinner, a few drinks, and maybe a movie, then there's this motel that has those vibrating beds and dirty movies that I thought we could stay at and then in the morning eat breakfast at The House of Pancakes.'" By now Grace was standing in front of Joey and fighting a smile from her face. He was leaning back against the front desk. Joey couldn't keep eye contact, which didn't mean anything to Grace because she could still embarrass him, even after all their intimate times together.

"However. I don't think that I can see you anymore." Grace no longer had to fight a smile, and her cheek muscles dropped. "You see." Grace slapped him, one hit. As quickly as she brought her hand up, she just as quickly dropped it back down to her side. "Oww." Holding one hand against the sting on his face, Joey looked at Grace in disbelief. He never expected her to hit him. Scream at him maybe, but don't hit him. He watched in slow motion as she prepared to speak or yell. Her shifting eyes were calculating some vicious assault, and her jaw was sliding forward, her lips were parting, and her teeth were becoming visible.

"Let me get this fucking straight. I haven't seen you in a year, and the first night we're together, you stick your little dick in every hole in my body, pleasing yourself because you're married to a woman that couldn't turn on a prison inmate. You leave before morning. I don't hear from you for two days. Then you tell me you don't want to see me anymore." Joey opened his mouth to talk, but Grace wouldn't let him. "You goddamn prick."

"I am very sorry, but."

"Yeah, you're sorry and ridiculous."

"Look, Grace."

"Don't you 'look Grace' me. I've been seeing and giving the best of who I am. And." Grace's voice split. Losing her composure, she turned away for a moment. Taking a deep breath, Joey could hear her tremble.

"Grace, baby." Joey reached toward her.

"Oh no you don't." Grace turned back around to face him, now with tears in her eyes, and raising her finger up again to stop him. "I thought you were a little better, but you're no different than any other guy. You know you parade around here like some grand master of the literary world, but I couldn't finish reading one of your books. You write like someone would expect from an English professor, pretentious and overcompensating for originality. Your characters are one dimensional and very unbelievable. I mean come on, what self-proclaimed literary writer has a character who boxes professionally until he's thirty, then because he has a life altering experience where he kills a guy in the ring, goes on to study medicine and eventually becomes chief neurologist at St Johns, and demonstrates the personality of Patch Adams. Give me a fucking break." The tears in her eyes and the crackle in her voice made Grace's words all the more sincere and potent.

"Come on, Grace, there's no call for that." Joey could take her saying that he had a small dick, but he worked hard all of his life on his writing. It's what he wanted to do ever since he was in junior high. Even if his acting stint had received better reviews and more offers, it wouldn't have stopped his writing. And Grace knew that was always an exposed nerve for him.

"Do you know that anyone that has confided in me and read your books, couldn't finish them because they found them dull and arrogant. I think the only reason you got published was because you're a college professor and probably fucked some coed that took one of your classes and went on to become an agent after graduation, perhaps promising to represent you if you gave her an A in the course.

"Actually, all of my agents have been male."

"Well, let's face it, honey, I've slept with you. You're not exactly bubbling with male testosterone." Grace, near to where she was sitting in class stepped over, grabbed her notebook and her purse that was hanging on the back of her chair. The strap fell, catching on the back rest. She flicked it quickly to get it unhooked, but it was still caught. Joey walked toward her to say something. Frustrated, she yanked her purse, bringing the light chair up in the air with it. Joey saw it in time to raise an arm to block it, but the way it spun through the air, one of the other legs landed against his temple near his eye. He staggered a little and braced himself on one of the desks. Grace almost asked if he was alright, but instead she unhooked her purse and dropped the chair to the floor. Joey was holding his face again. Grace marched out of the room. She tried slamming the door behind her, but it was on a plunger and could only shut slowly on its own or with steady pressure.

Tom found Joan alone, just coming out of her room and heading to the main dorm for lunch time. Either to see if people were going out or just to socialize with some eating peanut butter and crackers or heating up water in the microwave for noodles. Joan had on a plain, faded denim shirt and faded blue jeans to match; even the gray in her hair seemed to match— faded, worn, and comfortable now. Her shirt was hanging down, untucked. It made her look sexy. It made a lot of women look sexy. Tom wondered why women usually feel the need to tuck in their shirts. Was it to show their hips, or a flat stomach? They were right years ago: showing less is sexier. Joan didn't just look sexy, she looked so together. She didn't pile on accessories like most women do as they get older, more jewelry, more pins, high hair, more makeup. She looked like the type of woman for any situation, just as secure at a theme park as a fancy restaurant. She proved it the night before with dinner, then dancing with Noah and the other old man that Tom never got his name. Joan proved how classy she was in the way she could dance with the old man and his cane and still display elegance.

"Hey"

"Hi Tom." Joan looked over Tom like a mother.

"Being how things didn't work out so well last night, you want to go out again tonight?"

"Well, I think things worked out really well last night. I had a wonderful time. Especially when we all went dancing. I had three men that wouldn't let me sit down for a minute. What girl wouldn't like that sort of attention. But I've been thinking."

"Ah oh." Tom tried to be lighthearted.

"Yeah Tom. I'm sorry but I don't think we should take this any farther.

You're a beautiful man and well."

"This isn't just because Noah saw us together visit?"

"No, heavens no."

"The age differences?"

"Well, I can't say that that isn't part of it. But there's a lot more to it than that. Please respect my decision and just leave it at that."

"I do respect your decision, Joan. And I respect you immensely. However, it does hurt."

"I'm very sorry Tom." Tom took a deep breath and smiled.

"Would you at least let me still take you out to dinner again some night before we leave? Just the two of us?"

"I would love that, but not tonight." They hugged one another. Tom took a whiff of her perfume.

"Um, you are a handsome lady, Joan."

"Oh, stop," she said.

There were more people at the main dorm at lunch time than there were the two days prior. The expense to go out was becoming too much for most everyone's budget for one reason. For another, a lot of the attendees were starting to get serious on their preparation for the agents and editors. And also, the weather outside looked too unpredictable. Storms were coming and going all morning. There were black clouds, lightning strikes, and heavy winds, then turn to an overcast calm. The local weather station kept changing its forecast and upgrading to worse conditions. There were reports of tornados in rural areas not yet touching down in residential neighborhoods. No one believed that this kind of activity would last well into the evening. By then, surely the conditions had to subside.

When dinner rolled around, very few ventured into the city. Instead, most decided on eating the snacks that they kept in their rooms or shared to make some sort of meal with others if they could get willing participants. The lightning strikes returned in dramatic numbers, and the high winds came at almost unnatural levels. One large oak toppled in front of the main entrance to the classrooms. Campus maintenance removed some of the large tree, but not enough to clear the opening for the doors, they would have to come back the following day to cut the rest up and remove the trunk. Plus, they had other problems to attend to with the storm, particularly on the main campus. Abigail was more determined than ever to hold her seance that evening, believing that there had become a combined effort in the spirit world to stop her. It looked as though she would have a large turnout, with everyone being reluctant to leave campus. And that would be helpful, so long as she could get others to support her belief. She would have to spend the early part of the evening socializing and being more affable and approachable than she was in the past. She knew many people's feelings toward her and had to make a strong effort to change that. But Abigail had little confidence in that area, ever since her daughter disowned her. Progressively, it was becoming harder for her to make normal connections with people.

Abigail was one of the few that ventured out, petrified the whole time that a spirit would try and crash her car in order to keep her from doing the seance that evening. So, she focused her thoughts on insignificant things in order to hide her intentions the entire time she went out to Kentucky Fried Chicken and came back with several buckets of the Colonel's original recipe for anyone that wanted some. One way of doing this was by inviting others to go along with her to help distract her. She asked anyone from the large crowd gathered in the lobby. No one answered immediately. Jeff Hermann and Julie Kenyara seated closest to her at the time, seemed almost obligated to. Julie almost made the excuse that she had some work to do on her manuscript, but she didn't. Besides, the electrical storm made it too hard for her to concentrate. Most everyone was putting their writing on hiatus for the time being, worried that the storm may cause a surge or outage that could cause them to lose or damage files on their computers. A few were writing on paper, but the whole feeling of the evening was waiting to see what everyone else was going to do and to bounce ideas off of other presentations they wanted to give on the upcoming weekend.

Oscar was spending all his time with Josslyn and vice versa. They shared their stories and could hardly criticize one another. They loved to hear the other read and were doing so with a great deal of animation, amusing themselves with imitations and accents. They took turns pretending to be an agent or editor while the other tried to sell their story.

"Well, I really appreciate you giving me the

opportunity to read your work, but unfortunately because of the large number of submissions we have already, our agency doesn't give a shit whether your story is good or not," Josslyn said trying to keep a straight face while Oscar was acting like he was about to cry. He quivered his bottom lip and blinked rapidly with a devastated look on his face.

"But, but, please your highness. If only you could give me this one chance.

You won't regret it."

"My goodness! do not grovel, dear peasant. Because I am so kind, I shall employ other means."

"And what might that be, my lady?"

"You shall be my sexual servant." Josslyn was instantly paralyzed by what she said. Oscar read her sudden embarrassment. He scrambled, trying to think of something to say to shake off the awkwardness.

"Then I shall wear the position with great honor." Josslyn was dumbfounded, unable to return with any witty remark.

"Sorry, I didn't mean to say that." Josslyn was sitting on the edge of the bed, and Oscar was at the desk nearest the window. She had turned her head away from him and was running her finger back and forth along the creases that the covers made from her weight.

"I'm not sorry," Oscar replied, getting up from the chair, taking a step toward Josslyn, and leaning down to kiss her on top of the head. But Josslyn didn't notice. Just when she worked up the courage to face him, she turned too quickly and bumped Oscar's jaw, causing his teeth to slam together.

"UMMM!" Oscar held his hand over his mouth.

"Oh, my God. Are you alright?" Josslyn stood up and put her hands on Oscar. "I think I chipped a tooth."

"I am very, very sorry."

"Don't worry about it. It wasn't your fault." Oscar spit the piece of tooth into his hand. It was a triangle piece, almost one eighth of an inch across at its widest point. Oscar curled his upper lip back for Josslyn to look at. "Does it look bad?" he asked, keeping his upper lip raised. His top left front tooth was broken on the corner next to the other front tooth. Josslyn thought of Mike Tyson. Josslyn waited too long to answer, and Oscar stepped over to the mirror above the sink in the room. He looked momentarily in shock, with his upper lip still curled back and eyes widened in disbelief. Josslyn saw his reaction and felt even worse.

"Oh, I am so sorry, Oscar. I'm always doing terrible things to you." Josslyn looked as though she was about to start crying.

"No, you're not. They're accidents, and it's more my fault than it is yours" Oscar put his arms around her cautiously, making sure she noticed him before he did so. "Hey, after the seance tonight, you wanna go out for a little bit?"

"Sure. That sounds great."

When Oscar and Josslyn walked through the door to the main lobby, Dorothy gave Oscar a questionable look but smiled and turned back toward the table to grab a piece of chicken. It appeared the majority of Red Creek writers were there. Even Warren was in the room tonight, having missed the play the night before. The attractive couple that made an odd entrance earlier that morning introduced themselves to Oscar and Josslyn. They had been standing by the door, appearing ostracized by the rest of the room. In truth, they didn't eat meat, so they didn't partake in Abigail's offering and were trying to stay clear of everyone else struggling to get a leg or a breast before they were all gone.

"Hi, my name is Adam, and this is my wife, Kate." Adam cupped Oscar's hand like the grip for an arm-wrestling match. He swaggered his shoulders like a rapper and Oscar couldn't help looking up at someone who could explain his behavior. Dorothy had turned back just in time to see part of it. The puzzled look on Oscar's face made Dorothy want to burst out in laughter, but she had a mouth full of food and instead almost sprayed it. However, she stopped herself, looking as though she got something caught in her throat, and regained her composure.

"Excuse me," Oscar said and escorted Josslyn to the table. Oscar leaned over and whispered into Warren's ear, who was sitting at the table. "What's with Vanilla Ice over there?" Warren looked over his shoulder to see the estranged couple standing there.

"Oh, you mean the second generation of insider trading? They ended up at the wrong conference, thinking this was a retreat for the illegitimate children of the Kennedy's." Oscar smiled, forgetting about his tooth. "What happened to your tooth?"

"Nothing. . .I walked into a door."

"Alright. If you say so."

Josslyn sat down by Katrina. They were about to greet each other when the lights flickered. Warren shouted across the dorm toward Abigail, who had just come out of the center room attached to the lobby, needing to use the toilet because of her nerves.

"I hope you got those candles ready, Abigail. Looks like we're going to need them before the seance." Abigail went back into the room and back out with a two-foot square box filled with two-inch diameter cylindrical candles. The box was heavy, indicated by the small, hurried steps Abigail took to get it to the table. Jeff Hermann and Dorothy walked over to give her a hand.

"Where do you want us to put them," Jeff asked seemingly very interested to see the seance get started.

"Oh, just kind of evenly around the room on anything stable," Abigail replied flailing her hands in different directions. Before anyone had time to grab candles out of the box, the lights flickered and went out for a few seconds. Only long enough for a couple "shit's" and "damn it's", then they turned back on again, coinciding with lightning flashes outside.

"We better hurry," Dorothy said in a raised voice hoping others would lend a hand, but they were already approaching the table. Warren helped in lighting the candles as attendees pulled them out of the box. Some didn't offer any sort of support, either being too skeptical or finding the whole thing ridiculous, such as Adam and Kate. Others wished instead that the power wasn't so untrustworthy, so they could return to their manuscripts, like Barnell who since the evening before was writing incessantly. Then, there was Denise who found it all very amusing and quaint, and Julie who was just showing an interest to fit in. Lenny Garring was there for the three other reasons and could care less if he fit in.

Half the candles in the box was lit when the

power finally went out. Everyone paused, thinking it would come on again in a few seconds, but after several seconds more, they realized that it wasn't a test that time. But there were enough candles lit now that it was easy to finish displaying the others. Everyone began talking again, but in a softer tone. The candlelight had a way of doing that.

"You'd think the University would have some sort of auxiliary power," Jim said to Grace, both sitting next to the windows in the cushioned chairs.

"Well, obviously not, unless it just hasn't kicked in yet."

"We don't have any sort of secondary power at the University where I teach in Indiana," Lenny interjected, standing by and overhearing the conversation. Lenny looked and acted like Bear Bryant and taught his English as though he were coaching. "It happened in the middle of my class one time, and just when all the students were dismissed from the campuses, the power came back on. I can't imagine however, the power staying off for too long, being in the city like this."

"That made me realize something. Shouldn't we be listening to the radio to find out what's going on," Grace stated with minor concern.

"That's a good idea." Jim got up, went to his room, and came back with a green Phillips radio having the CD and cassette players. "It has fresh batteries in it, so it should last a while." There was an extremely large thunderclap that sounded as though it was immediately above the main dorm, quite a few of the attendees jumped. Besides the enormity of it that seemed out of the ordinary, no one remembered seeing a lightening flash prior to it.

"May I have your attention, please?" Abigail's voice barely traveled beyond a few people standing next to her, fortunately Warren was one of them. He stood up.

"May we have your attention, please?" Warren was able to project his voice farther than most, clearly and confidently. It was something he developed while in the service. Being drafted as a shy kid, the Marine Corps or Vietnam had little patience for the soft-spoken.

Everyone turned to see Warren standing next to Abigail. The yellow and orange hue somehow showed the coarseness of their two years of life experience and sadness, covered only by their stoic and complacent stares. But the candlelight depicted everyone differently. Honestly maybe, I wasn't quite sure at the time.

"Abigail, I'm sure you'd like to get this started," Warren announced, smiling at her. "And I myself am curious to see what business this ghost has with us." Warren said it with sincerity, but most everyone who knew Warren believed in this whole affair about as much as they did. Also, the few that believed or wanted to believe, such as May and Julie, who would never admit it, sided with Abigail and her intentions only because they didn't know better.

"Okay, what I'd like for everyone to do, because there are so many people here, is to form a circle around the lobby and join hands. The connection is very important during the séance, so I beg that no one separate themselves from the person next to them." Everyone started milling around the room to find a spot. Some were finding seats, while others intended to stand. "I've asked Warren to remain disconnected from the group in order to carry out certain tasks. However, I need one other volunteer to remain outside the circle. And it should be someone who doesn't have much belief in what is going on here tonight, which will probably be hard to do." A few people laughed, and several were surprised to see that side of Abigail. "Jim, would you like to volunteer?" There were a couple more laughs.

"Sure, I'll…"

"I'll do it, Abigail," Elaine interrupted. "If that's okay with you, Jim?"

"No, fine, be my guest." It was good for Abigail because Jim believed more than he let on. And he wanted to believe more than he let on. The only problem with others besides Abigail that either believed to some degree or wanted to, is that it's all rooted in the thought that they are there to help

Abigail send the spirit "into the light", or onto an afterlife where they will "find peace." That's a bunch of bullshit. If anyone has any level of expertise in contacting the dead, simply to "purge them" or rather send them to another realm, in essence, what they are really doing is ostracizing that spirit from being welcomed into their lives. It only sends the spirit away packing from that area. This is the worst form of séance anyone can do. It's like The Exorcist, well not that dramatic, you're not pissing off demonic possession, but you are pissing off a spirit that just wants to belong. If Abigail would've held a séance to just call up spirits to visit, that would've been nice. Instead, she wanted to hold a séance to get rid of someone she didn't even know.

While everyone stood around the outside of the room and talked in low voices, Abigail went to the center where Warren and Elaine were seated next to a small coffee table with bottles of water and towels. She instructed them on different things to do should the situation arise. Warren looked half interested only to be courteous. And Elaine looked more interested only to be more courteous. After that, she stood up and addressed all the others.

"One last thing before we get started. If you see something this evening those surprises you… and it might, please remember to keep your hands connected at all costs." Some people grinned, and some others fought back laughter with a cough or clearing of their throat. All, however, were kind enough to leave Abigail's speech uninterrupted. "The presence may inhabit someone's body next to you. Whatever you do, do not let go of them." There was some small laughter by a few, and when it wasn't carried on by the others, it faded nervously. Abigail was unaffected. She was determined, and besides, she's been laughed at for many years now. She had also been laughed at by people in public who later came to see her in private with desperate and pleading looks, their eyes filled with tears or wiped away moments before they entered her home. She was often their last vestige of hope.

Abigail walked over and stood in front of the door at the opposite end of the room from the refrigerator, microwave, and coffee pot. She was prepared, no earrings, no jewelry; a one-piece, light weight dress, beige, and white, and only sandals on her feet. She stood between Joan and Tom. That was a comfort for her to have Joan next to her, and the biggest reason she decided to take that end of the room. Joan was the only other attendee she felt close to other than Warren, who to her was just a good Samaritan and confidant. She had to pick one end or the other to see everyone clearly if need be.

She took their hands and then asked everyone to please do the same.

bigail took a deep breath, and when it seemed she had taken in all she could, she sucked in a couple more mouthfuls like children getting ready to see who could stay under water the longest. When she released her air, energy surged through every connecting body in that room. It was the equivalent of using CPR and having it work. I knew something was going to happen then. This wasn't smoke and mirrors; she was going to be able to make contact or wreak havoc.

"I welcome all that are living, bodies still connected with the soul, connected in our lives to one another, walking this earth and leaving footprints." Somewhere behind her words, Abigail's voice had a dizzying hum to it, unnatural and so unexplainable that anyone would've said that it didn't exist. "Join me, everyone in this room. Close your eyes and breathe. Feel the air that the living feel, your lungs expanding in your chest. Feel your heart and pulse beat in rhythm with those around you. Feel your blood circulate–vital and rich. Test your senses as you stand or sit in this room. What do you smell at the moment? Take a deep breath…What do you hear at the moment, besides my voice? Listen. What do you feel at the moment you touch your neighbors' hand? This is all life around you." The door burst open behind Abigail. Everyone opened their eyes, most in disbelief. Still, everyone remained holding hands. Abigail looked over her shoulder, confused and angry.

"Excuse me but I just wanted to let everybody know that the power is going to be off for some time." It was campus security, a young black man from the area, given his accent. "Apparently, they're having this problem in town with a lot of power lines down 'n' stuff." No one responded. A little nervously now, looking into Abigail's one eye that seem focused on him impatient and angry, he added, "I just wanted to let ya' all know." He glanced around the room. "What's going on?"

"We're having a seance, young man," Joan offered with a smile.

"Oh, well, instead of bringing back the dead, you might want to try bringing back the power." He smiled impishly at his own joke, but no one laughed. "Okay, well, I've got to go tell the other dorms." He let the door go. It closed slowly, allowing Joan to hear the young man as he walked away shaking his head, "fuckin' writers."

I felt his interruption refreshing and relaxing, but Abigail continued, and I knew she would. First, she paraphrased what she said before, and the hum still trailed her words, but it became fiercer.

"Spirit from Wisconsin, you are not a part of life anymore. You are broken from all attachments. You are disconnected. You are left to observe, watch, wait, and appreciate." Wait a minute. What the fuck does she mean by "observe, watch, wait, and appreciate"? What made her think that the living had the exclusive rights to interact. Her hum exhausted me, but still I was able to get in her face and yell, Ahhh! It would stop her only for a moment. So, I did it again and again. No one else seemed to notice, but I know she was aware of it. That smug bitch. I wanted her to stop talking so goddamn badly, and tried thinking of ways to divert her attention. But her voice was tiring, and she put out so much energy in that room.

No one wanted me there, I knew that. But I wasn't about to let that cunt get rid of me. I deserved to be there just as much as anyone else. I had to be there for my brother. He never made me feel like I didn't belong.

"You must move on spirit. There are others waiting for you." Who? Who the hell is waiting for me I thought. My wife? She's been fucking the pharmacist now for six months and before that it was the electrician who did our wiring when we put on the new addition.

I wasn't about to let that bug-eyed witch cancel my membership, though it was getting tiring to be there. Things were becoming blurry and surrealistic, which is the best way I can explain them. Some objects remained solid while others became transparent, as if I could see them broken down into particles, molecules, and then atoms. I didn't seem to be able to trust my movements. But then there was a break, like a vacuum sucked out all the disorientation. Everything was clear again, and the source drew my attention so quickly that I knew I had to act just as fast to keep Abigail from trying to evict me.

Adam let go of Kate's hand so he could scratch his nose. Abigail sensed it right away. She opened her eyes and screamed, "NO!" I penetrated Adam. Or I took over his body if that makes more sense and seems less vulgar. I don't know if I can explain how I did it. I think it was such a desperate desire for me at the time that it came to me on pure instinct. I've seen it in movies and read about being possessed before, but I didn't really think it was possible. After all, I don't think I'm demonic by any means. And besides, where does the other soul go? There didn't seem to be anything in the way when I got into Adam, and it felt as workable as being back in my own body, though not very natural, and the smell of him made it uncomfortable. It wasn't B.O. or bad cologne. It was a personal smell that made the invasion feel slightly perverse. But it was a good rental, and I was about to drive it until it ran out of gas. I was pissed, and I wanted all the other wannabees to know it.

I stood and paused for a minute, and Abigail stared at me, and because of this, so did most everyone else. Or should I say they stared in my direction, uncertain who Abigail was really looking at. Kate tried grabbing my hand, but I slapped it away.

"Don't touch me, you frigid bitch." Just then, Denise let go, standing on the other side of me. "Yeah, you better let go too, you self-absorbed and overrated hack. What? You look shocked. You really don't think anybody but librarians read that shit you write, do you? I mean, who in their fucking right mind wants to read the memoirs of some unknown local stage actress that has the acting range of Lassie?" I walked toward Abigail. Warren and Elaine got up, as if to come to her aid.

"Everyone join hands," Abigail commanded the room shaking.

"You really don't think that's going to work now, do ya Abby?" Quite a few in the room believed that it was a hoax, and some were certain it wasn't. Warren and Elaine knew that Abigail couldn't have prearranged this. So, they were polarized on what action to take, waiting mainly to make sure that no one would hurt her. Warren stood next to Abigail with Elaine right behind him. I stepped up to within three feet of the trio…well, group. Joan and Tom were still standing on both sides of the witch, holding her hands. Her circle was still complete so I couldn't touch her and she knew it, but I had no intention of hurting her, physically that is. This wasn't in the least what was planned or thought could happen. She assumed I'd be drawn out, weakened, and pleading to be directed on some spiritual journey.

"Spirit, we are connected here. No body or means you take to assimilate…"

"Oh, shut the fuck up, will ya?" I leaned closer to Abigail, and Warren scooted a foot closer toward me. "What do you think you're going to do, Warren? Look at this body I've got, for Christ's sake!. I'm a lean green fighting machine. All that training in Vietnam doesn't stand a chance against this well- defined and oiled, black belt certified, could care less if you served your country, and I got my education at an ivy league college only because my parents could afford it, body. Life sucks, doesn't it when selfish pricks like Adam here get all the breaks, although you've busted your ass only to lose your job and served your country in a war where all you got was being called white trash and a baby fucker.

You ended up with a back that won't allow you to carry a twelve pack without being in pain. You live in a trailer that isn't wide enough to fit your obese mother. You have no retirement plan or savings to fall back on. And yet, like an ignorant fool, you think those tender war stories where you watched your buddies die spitting blood and telling you to let their loved ones know how much they cared for them are going to get you out of debt?"

Warren tried to hit me, but I could see it coming. I didn't want to hurt him because I really like him, but I think even without Adam's body, I could've deflected the punch. Warren hasn't been in a fight in a couple decades, and I don't think he realized how slow he'd become. I spun him around and pushed him away, into Elaine, who caught him as he stumbled over the arm rest of a chair. It was simple enough that no one felt the urgency to break from the circle and help out, not even Oscar, who seemed ready to come to anyone's aid.

"Adam!" Kate shouted as if to keep me from doing anything else.

"Honey, Adam ain't here. As a matter of fact, I don't think there was anyone at the wheel when I got here. Then again, there's probably no one driving you either.

Warren, too bad the War Correspondant didn't come to the party, he could've shown you a few things. It's insult to injury Warren, a new age. You don't receive credit for your deeds or actions. Just look at Julie over there. The girl who has everything but a personality. Born of privilege the closest she'll ever feel to being threatened is this moment here."

"Alright, that's enough."

"Oh my, will you look at this? Joan of Arc speaks. What? Do you feel noble and invincible because you turned down the chance to fuck Tom, mister California cool? The only reason you didn't screw him is because you knew if it went poorly and he could get past the drooping tits, flat waffle ass, and rotten pussy, you'd never be able to meet with your woman's church group again and feel like the so called attractive one. And you know goddamn well that's the only thing you've got left to give you any feeling of self-worth."

"Hey!"

"Hey what? Don't even let me get started on you, Tom. If I told all the women here what you look like when you beat off, I think they'd be less anxious to hop in bed with you." Of course, I had to give a demonstration, squeezing my eyes shut and crinkling my nose. "Even Grace. Besides, your endurance record leaves a lot to be desired, but then, isn't that really why you wanted to have sex with Joan isn't it? You figured that because of her age, she wouldn't have any high expectations and maybe she'd overlook your short comings."

It amazed me at that time no one approached me or wanted to argue. Many seemed to be enjoying the show, while others were just afraid that I'd expose their secrets. A couple were just disgusted, especially regarding the remarks about the rotten pussy and beating off simulation.

"So, you want to get rid of me, do ya Broom Hilda?"

"Spirit, please."

"Ahh for fuck sakes, quit with the spirit shit already. Will ya? I have a name and it's Jordan. I feel I know you so well, we should, after all, be on a first name basis. Don't you agree? Come on say something. Cat got your tongue. You can't incriminate yourself—I already know everything there is to know about you. You have no friends, your husband left you for something that would get his dick up, and your daughter is so embarrassed she tells all her friends that you've died of cancer. And I know the only thing you've got that keeps you going is feeling needed by those poor, ignorant, out of work mountain hicks that come to dear Abbey for some pathetic potion they think will turn their luck around and get them that winning lotto ticket so they can buy their dream double wide trailer home. Something I'm sure Warren has prayed to the good old Baptist Lord for many times."

Even in my anger, it hurt to see Abigail fighting her tears, not wanting to cry and show that I told the truth. And I should've stopped, but they wanted to get rid of me. I didn't want to get rid of them. I liked all of them, believe it or not.

"And so, who's next? Josslyn? Buzz? Oscar? Yeah, don't even let me get started on you, brother. How about."

"How about me?" May broke the circle, getting up with her cane. "Sure, Mother Teresa, the martyr."

"That's right, Jordan. Are you gonna tell me how lonely I am? How I hang on to every single contact as if it were my reason for living. Well, you're not going to tell me something I don't already know. Or are you going to tell me how much I'm wasting my time trying to get something published that no one wants to read coming from an inarticulate old lady, but I come to these conferences only as a chance to get out of my dingy apartment and all those stray cats because I can't even get my own kids to visit me? Is that what you're going to tell me? Well, then, aren't you a regular Sherlock Holmes. Don't you think that there isn't a person here that either already knows that or assumes it? Some insightful apparitions you turned out to be." Yeah, that's what I was going to tell her. I felt numb and defenseless against her slow, unsteady pace. Her stare behind those thick, distorting glasses no longer made her comical but compelling. "What are you hurting from, dear, and why are you really here?"

"I read your manuscript, Jordan. You're here for the same reason we all are. You're lost just like the rest of us," Warren interjected. I didn't expect that from him. That's where he was the night before when everyone else went to the play. "I'm sorry about your brother, pal. You changed the names in your story, but it was really about you, wasn't it? Your manuscript isn't fiction at all." I should've left at that moment, but I didn't. I was stumped and still hurt. The confusion frustrated me.

"Everyone's sorry. Everyone's always been sorry. My brother was the only good thing in my life, and all I ever got was I'm sorry. What the fuck good is that? Vietnam took him away and never brought him back. They never found him. The one person who ever made me feel like I belonged in my entire life. And the fucking idiots lost him. You'd think in death I'd see him, but I haven't seen anyone. Not a soul." I laughed at my own joke, hoping to keep from crying, but it didn't help. "You see, I loved my brother sooo much. He's what made my childhood so wonderful and then so horrible." And yeah, I cried, but I think it was less from the loss of my brother than from suddenly realizing that the rest of my life, since that single tragedy at the age of twelve, has been stymied because I was too afraid to care deeply.

Unnoticed, May had worked her way in front of me. She wrapped her arms around me just above the waist and hugged. I could see that short old lady, but I couldn't feel her. And I wanted to. I wanted to be reminded. The pressure was there, but no senses really registered anything, like being injected on every square inch of my body with Novocaine and high on Oxycontin. Worse than that, it felt perverted being in Adams body, like some forbidden sex. I don't know—maybe that's why you always see a body possession as demonic. I imagine demons could only tolerate this for so long.

Abigail stepped up to my side, grabbed my arm, arched herself over May and kissed me on the cheek. Still no sensation, but the observation was appreciated.

"I'm sorry," she said with glazed eyes. Those that hadn't already, the rest around the room broke chain. Joan and some others, including Adam's wife Kate, came toward me to show a little tenderness. I didn't belong there anymore. I made a point, made a fool of myself, insulted some good people, and invaded someone else's body. I left Adam. Wherever he was, I'm sure he wanted his body back.

aaa, what's going on? Why are you people touching me? Kate, honey!" It was only a second of startled looks before everyone realized that Adam was

back. He lifted his hands off May as if he were trying to avoid poison ivy.

"I'll explain it all to you in a little bit," Kate assured Adam. Everyone near him turned away, and anyone who only watched was still doing the same, surprised by Adam's reaction.

"I preferred when he was possessed," May mumbled, shuffling back to her chair. A few were still skeptical that it was all prearranged, like Jeff Hermann. A couple of the new attendees were cautious, not knowing much about the background of the people I insulted. Many knew that something extraordinary happened, and it may have been the most amazing thing they ever saw. Then there were a few who knew what really happened. The crowd talked with whom they felt closest to, pairing off or in threes. No one felt that they had to give a speech to the others. An explanation was left for each individual, believer or not, to argue, embellish, deny, or simply never speak of again. The lights flickered for a moment, stopped, flickered again, and came on, along with the refrigerator and somebody's television who left their door open in the second-floor balcony.

A couple hurrays seemed trivial to the event that unfolded prior. Jim remained dumbfounded and awestruck, still sitting in the same place he was when the I started. Oscar walked over to him while Josslyn seemed to be making friends with Katrina.

"Hey…Jim, you okay?" Oscar sat down beside him. "Yeah, I think so."

"You look lost, man."

"I feel lost at the moment."

"That was some pretty amazing stuff."

"You know, Oscar, I never thought in my entire life that anyone was watching me."

"You're not worried that some spirit caught you beating off, are you?"

"No, nothing like that. I guess I just never felt as though there was anything there. You know? I thought things were simple, that there wasn't any other dimension to us other than flesh, bones, and pulsating neurons."

"Didn't you ever wonder about that as a kid? Or need to sleep with the light on because you were worried a ghost might get you?"

"No. It all just seemed silly and unfathomable to me."

"What about when your dad died?" Oscar wanted to take back the question, but it was already out there. Jim's dad committed suicide when he was thirteen. It came up in a late-night conversation at one of the conferences when Oscar, Jim, and Elaine were talking about growing up.

"I just figured he was gone, that's all."

"I'm sorry, Jim."

"Yeah, me too…You know you really need to get that tooth fixed after this conference."

Not knowing where to go, I stayed, obviously and continued to watch everyone. What else could I do. I don't even know how I got to this conference, so I had no clue how to get anywhere else. What seems to motivate me in any direction are relationships, contacts, and my desires. At first, I worried that those who believed to some degree in what happened would become too cautious and apprehensive about carrying on with their normal routines. Their awareness and thinking of me made it almost as uncomfortable as not being wanted. Yet still, I was drawn to be around them. If anything, though everyone became a little more uninhibited. Except for Tom, but then Joan changed that. That evening, in fact. When she went to his room he accused her of pity, but the perfume she was wearing, and that cotton blouse made him believe that she was sincere in saying that she wanted to make love.

Everyone slept the best they could that evening. However, Adam and Kate slept randomly, dozing for minutes then waking with worry or to finish a thought. Adam was afraid he would be "possessed" again, and Kate spent the night hoping. Never having seen Adam cry before was refreshing, and she was pleased by it, and it was disconcerting to her that he didn't remember anything that went on. I suppose I should've been flattered, but one thing the afterlife confirms is that beauty is only skin deep. As for Abigail, she fell asleep holding her daughter's picture. It's when she was fourteen–the year she left her mom. It was a school picture and in no way displayed a disgruntled child–anything but. She was smiling, showing her teeth top and bottom, as if she were enjoying some friendly teasing with the person behind the camera. She had full, happy cheeks like her mother would've had if life were easier. She was lively, and her energy transcended out of the picture, touching anyone who saw it, making them wonder what she was smiling at and wishing they were in on the joke. If there was anyone I needed to apologize to, it was Abigail. But she thought of plans for her return home that night in order to win back her daughter's love. And if she applied herself to that the way she did in exercising demons, I would say she had a very good chance.

Josslyn and Oscar spent the night together talking in her room. By the time they both worked up the courage to embrace, they were both too tired, so Josslyn fell asleep with her head on Oscar's chest and her arm across his waist. Liz and Beverly called home to tell their husbands what happened during the seance but telling the story to someone who wasn't there made skepticism too easy, and neither of their husbands wanted to appear naive, especially knowing that their wives were fiction writers and exaggerated often to liven up parties or cookouts.

Nighttime's were the hardest for me, especially that night. The inactivity and the few conscientious attendees still awake or caressing a lover didn't seem enough to occupy me. And my worry became that several people would leave the next morning because of the seance. Their indecisive thoughts were too much to decipher, making it dizzying to follow. I could tell, though, that many were inspired by the evening, with plans to incorporate it into their current stories or use it as the premise of an entirely different novel. The following morning, after Jim rushed out of his room again only to find the coffee already made, Joey narrated the story to Noah like

Melville, giving the background and mannerisms of all the characters before tying them together in one catastrophic climax. He told it with such excitement and animation that even Grace sat with her legs drawn to her chest, sipping her coffee, absorbing every detail as though she were at home during the middle of the day watching her soaps. I, or rather Adam, appeared like a bitter and then compassionate White Whale, and Abigail as an obsessive and then misguided Ahab. Warren obviously was Queeequeg, May was Starbuck, and it seemed as though Joey set himself up to be easily mistaken for Ishmael.

Sessions for the day were cancelled, not only because of the downed tree in front of the union hall where the classes are held, but because everyone felt the need to put what they witnessed in context as well as polish their manuscripts for representatives from literary agencies and publishing houses, which I was happy to see. That meant that everyone wanted to stay. The bad weather left during the night, and the new day was partly to mostly cloudy with moderate winds. There was a sense of community among the writers, not like the first day when most wanted to go to lunch together, but much more than that because they all had something unique to share, whether they mocked it or not. They all dug deeper into their pockets, decided to put more on their credit cards, and even extended charity, with Kate forcing Adam to pick up the tab for May, Buzz, Bobbie, and even Jeff, who rode with them out to lunch. Jeff annoyed the group through most of the meal with his conspiracy theories on how it was just a hoax and tried getting Adam to admit he was in on it. Adam wished it was a hoax, for one reason that he had no recollection and it made him uncomfortable, and for another reason that he didn't like to hear about the way he behaved, primarily the part about crying.

Kate thought Adam was horribly concrete and practical, dealing only in facts. When she first met him, it was charismatic, being able to start conversations with anyone at any time on most any topic, due to his wealth of trivial knowledge. At the time they started trying to adopt, she realized his emotional limitations. Still, she liked being married to him, knowing how to make money, plus she knew they looked good together as a couple and a lot of her friends envied her. And yeah, I delved a little deeper into her thoughts to discover that. But it wasn't terribly hard. She'd been questioning their relationship ever since the seance.

For dinner that day almost everybody ordered out, following the trend of a few that started with an early meal. Many of the writers started drinking early and didn't want to risk the driving in the city. Dorothy took Katrina with her and brought back Chinese orders and some subs. A few ordered pizzas and had it delivered. Two thirds of the Red Creek Writers group were in the main dorm lobby by 7PM.

Abigail hadn't been seen all day, except by Warren who stopped by her room at noon to see how she was doing. He let several of the others know that she was fine when they asked about her. When she walked into the lobby no one could keep themselves from looking at her. She was different and less hurried, timid because of the eyes on her, but it was the first time anyone remembered seeing her in slacks and pull over polyester shirt. She looked less a witch and more like one of the female nurses at the hospital, Oscar thought.

"Hey Abigail." There were several greetings as she walked by everyone on the lounge furniture and toward the table.

"Hi Abbey," Joan said. "Here, I saved you a chair." Actually, Tom was sitting next to her before she got up to go to the toilet.

"You wanna drink, young lady?"

"Sure, Noah, wine if you have any."

"Yes ma'am. Comin' right up. Chardonnay alright?"

"Sounds good." It seemed inappropriate to talk about the seance with Abigail there, so anyone who was talking about it before she came into the room went on to other discussions. Everyone noticed that Abigail looked weak, or at the final stage of recovering from a hangover when you're able to just now put food on your stomach. So, it was assumed that the spiritual battle was like that of The Exorcist, with Abigail being physically exhausted much the same way as Max Von Sydow. When Abigail believed that no one was paying attention to her she leaned forward and confessed to Joan. "I talked to my daughter today." Joan wanted to ask how it went, but instead gave Abigail her undivided attention. "She said she wants to meet me at the airport when I come home."

"Oh, that's wonderful, Abbey."

"Well, I don't think she's as enthusiastic as I am, but she did say she wanted to spend some time with me."

"Abbey, I'm so happy for you, honey."

"Thanks. I just hope I don't embarrass her."

"Don't say that. She misses her mom, and I think she's just beginning to realize how special you are."

"I appreciate that, Joan." Joan gave Abigail a hug.

"What's that Grace?" Barnell asked from the other side of the room, seeing Grace twirl a CD on her finger and walk over to Jim's radio and player, still in the lobby atop the refrigerator. She was in tight faded jeans, stocking feet, and an Ozzy Osbourne tee shirt, cut short to reveal her belly.

"A mix of some oldies to help liven this party." She put the CD in, adjusted the volume, grabbed a banana (also sitting on top of the fridge), turned around, and gave everyone an impish grin. A chorus of *"Paperback…paperback writer"* interrupted the room. But it was a pleasant interruption, and several people smiled immediately. Then Grace sang along with the Beatles classic.

"Dear Sir or Madam, will you read my book. It took me years to write, will you take a look. Based on a novel by a man named Lear, and I need a job, so I want to be a paperback writer. Paperback writer." Before the first stanza was through, Buzz, Elaine, Jim, and Dorothy joined in singing as Grace started walking provocatively around the room in a hammed-up parody of Marilyn Monroe and using a banana as a microphone. As the song continued, several others added their voices to the harmony. Grace ran her finger in a circle outlining Noah's bald spot, kissing him on the forehead, then moved on to Oscar and sat on his lap, then in passing swept her hand across Adams shoulder. In the last stanza, Grace kneeled in front of Barnell, who was sitting in one of the cushioned chairs. She moved in close, forcing his legs apart. His embarrassment was inescapable, reddening his ears and cheeks, near to the point of perspiration. This is what put Grace in her element–rubbing her hand along his leg, short of him reaching down to stop her.

"But I need a break, and I want to be a paperback writer. Paperback writer. Paperback writer. Paperback writer. Paperback writer. Paperback writer." There was applause, and Grace hopped up, giving quick curtsies like an eleven-year-old girl pleased with herself. She winked at Barnell, then moved the small coffee tables and ottomans out of the center of the room as David Gray's "We're Not Right" began to play. Grace pulled Warren out of his chair for a slow dance. Joey invited Abigail, Lenny courted Elaine, Kate forced her husband, and Joan nudged Tom. Josslyn kept telling Oscar that she didn't know how to dance, but halfway through the song she gave in. Oscar's style, strength, and experience made it impossible to tell that Josslyn had never danced before. Katrina worked up the nerve to ask a new first year attendee just before the song ended. Seeing her disappointment and wanting to get to know her, he kept her on the floor for the next song, "American Woman" by The Guess Who. I was glad to hear that it wasn't Lenny Cravitz's version.

Grace had a good selection of music, although I never did hear any Bowie, and the party was wonderful. I sensed that everyone had a good time. At one of the slow songs, Warren asked Denise to dance. She had been quiet since the night before, questioning herself more than any of the others that I observed. She accepted the dance, and they spoke little to one another, only asking each other how the writing was going.

Friday, everyone returned to the schedule of classes and their projects. Elaine, Joey, Lenny, Julie, and Tom all extended their sessions in preparation for the agent meeting Saturday. Denise regained her self- esteem, though lost motivation for her book idea. Although she kept her class short, she left herself open to listen and critique any of the writers who wanted a sounding board and some feedback, and several took her up on the offer. All the published authors gave reviews to the members of their group; some were hastily put together with apologies, while others were given a great deal of time, also with apologies. The general impression to me was, though this was the first conference that I've ever been to, that of friends trying to tell friends how to write. Elaine seemed to be the most talented at giving praise and encouragement while still delivering constructive criticism.

That late afternoon and evening, the agents arrived on different scheduled flights. Jim put their arrivals on the bulletin board a couple days prior, along with a sign-up list for attendees that cared to pick up and chauffeur, maybe go out for a coffee or drink and any other place they might be interested in. Following that, take them to their hotel room, where later the representatives would be taken to dinner. Warren and Elaine signed up together to escort one of the agents. Elaine also put a note under her name that if any of the unpublished writers would rather take her spot, she'd be more than happy to subside, which no one did. Jim suggested strongly to Warren that he didn't drive, knowing how uncomfortable his pickup would be for the New York types. Warren only protested to tease Jim but planned to let Elaine drive anyway.

The flight and jet lag (a couple of the agents had been traveling the country) made all the representatives chatty but absent minded. Elaine and Warren picked up Sharon Bent, a literary agent that handled mostly children's books, everything from the beginner to young adult. Occasionally, her agency would represent more adult context, but only if it fit mainstream culture and contemporary issues. She had two hobbies. One was buying first edition children's books, rare and unpopular, from old and used bookstores that didn't know their value. That's as long as they were still in good condition and had the original jacket. Warren was amused by Sharon's excitement when they took her around to the bookstores in Louisville. Already a cheap sell, the agent would still haggle over the price of a book with clerks.

Elaine was impartial, also being a book collector, but for her it was simply old editions of classics. Still, she could see the same irony that Warren saw. At one less popular bookstore Sharon walked out with a grocery bag full of hard cover books.

"Will you look at this. These people were sitting on a gold mine and didn't even know it," Sharon said, getting into the car.

"Yeah, will you look at that. All those books that no one wanted to read in the first place, and now they sell for twenty times their value to other people that won't read them either." Warren couldn't help himself, and Elaine wondered how far he was going to take it.

"There's a very lucrative market for these, Warren."

"So, if I write a bad children's book, I can make a lot of money?"

"Well, as long as you keep all the copies that don't sell, wait for them to go out of print, and then sit on them for a few years, yeah."

When Warren and Elaine took Sharon to her hotel and helped her carry her bags up to her room,

Sharon showed them her other hobby.

"Oh, you've got to see this." Excited, the agent's petite Calista Flockhart frame effortlessly tossed her large suitcase on the bed. She took out a yellow, octagonal plastic case, eighteen inches long, rolled it out on the table, and as if she had found King Solomon's mines, said "Ta da." Warren was puzzled. It was a hobby kit for making beaded bracelets and necklaces. It also had a section for making miniature notebooks that could fit in the palm, which Sharon had to demonstrate immediately. "Look at this. I made it for my husband. It's a notebook I made in the shape of a half heart." She opened it. "See, when you do that, it becomes a full heart." When Sharon sat it back down in one of the trays Warren looked over at Elaine and rolled his eyes. Elaine almost laughed but turned it into a cough instead. "What do you think?"

"Oh, that is very nice, how do ya do it?" Elaine thought she better interject before Warren.

"Well, it's really easier than it looks."

"Really," Warren had to say with a mocking astonishment that didn't register with the agent.

"Yeah, you'd be surprised." Sharon rolled the kit back up and put it in her suitcase.

"Do have any children, Sharon?" Warren asked.

"No, but we have two beautiful golden retrievers, Missy, and Max. Let me show you their pictures."

She spun around looking for her purse. "Now, where did I set my purse?"

"That's alright. We can look at them some other time. Warren and I better get going. I imagine you'd like to get some rest before dinner tonight."

"Where did I put my purse?"

Warren and Elaine left the room as Sharon still seemed distracted by looking for her purse, and as soon as they were out in the hallway Elaine started to laugh.

"Warren, your looks were killing me."

"Do you think maybe she forgot to take her medication?" Elaine stopped and doubled over in the hallway. She was laughing so hard she lost the ability to make any sound for the moment. "That lady is going to be pissed if she ever has any kids and the toddlers take over that hobby kit."

"St…op it."

"The bright side is, she'll have a lot of terrible first edition children's books for them to read."

"Stop…I mean it." It wasn't so much what Warren was saying, as it was the expressions he made that Elaine found hilarious. Warren had a very dry sense of humor, and with it he could maintain the perfect poker face, unflinching and deceivingly sincere.

Jim and Bobbie, along with members of Red Creek Writers who weren't attending the conference but were members of the organization, took the representatives out for dinner. The other members were lapsing authors and those who liked the title and could say they were on a board for writers but had professional careers whose salaries generally exceeded those of writers. Some of the more aggressive attendees followed the entourage to the restaurant, such as Grace, Julie, and Jeff, attempting to introduce themselves or partake in any witty banter that might lead to an introduction plug for their manuscript. However, in watching the group order their meals, everyone decided to themselves that it may not be the best timing.

All six of the representatives either knew or heard of each other in different dealings in their profession, and having plenty in common, seldom talked to the Red Creek Writers except to say pass the salt or pepper. They were like knights at a round table and all others were lowly squires. The literary royal guard kept their conversations, jokes and flailing of their arms mostly to themselves. One of them that dealt primarily in nonfiction material went so far as to whisper in the ear of another agent sitting on one side of him and then an agent on the other side. Both of which started laughing uncontrollably. I suppose I could've listened in on what they were saying but I didn't. It seemed unimportant to me when I saw how uncomfortable Jim and Bobbie were. Bobbie had been a veteran of the cold war, but this battle put her in an awkward position.

Following the agents return to their rooms for the night, Jim reported to many of the others that stayed behind and waited in the main dorm to hear what their chances might be during the interviews. He did imitations of all the representatives, entertaining a dozen of the attendees that evening. Jim had an uncanny ability to do caricatures when he wanted to. His satire made them all look like arrogant royalty. When he acted out one of the female agents, it was in the persona of an aristocratic matriarch, with the voice sounding like Dame Edna. He even wrapped a towel, someone had left on the back of a chair, into a bun on the top of his head. The performance even impressed Joey who was mostly hanging around to make amends with Grace and also to eventually find out if she really thought his writing, was crap. Jim needed the outlet and let go completely. Being director, this year made it hard for him to open up and relax in the way he did years prior.

Saturday morning Jim arranged a shuttle to take the representatives to breakfast, where they all were more docile, due mostly to the business deals and contacts they all needed to make on their cell phones. After breakfast they were taken to the campus in a conference building next to the dorms. This is where I started with my story, the representatives allowing themselves to be questioned about the marketing world for writers, and after the meeting to give interviews to those that still felt as though they could brave the patronizing professionals.

What did I say at the beginning? There's something about this all being a farce, I think. The agents told a few people that their story wasn't typically the kind of material they generally represented, then they told a few others to leave them a copy of their manuscript and they would look at it, and a few others they told to call another agent who they heard was looking for the kind of stuff they're writing. Two of the agents even told a handful of the wannabes that it looked as though it had potential, but they should run through another draft first and then seek a literary agent that will really work hard for them. A couple writers they amused even further and said that they would have their intern look at it, but right now, especially this time of year, the publishing houses are pretty much booked with what would be marketed, but if they wanted to try in the fall, they may have better luck.

Warren knew the drill, not just because he'd been here before, but because he used their personalities in his stories—deceitful characters that on initial introduction seem as harmless and trusting as a priest. The problem with professionals and the highly educated is that they become much more comfortable in their appearance when telling a lie or being deceptive. As if what they can get away with has become a challenge. Their concern becomes overly compassionate. And they know not to show anxiety when talking to writers, as though they could sit and talk for hours. They know how important it is to listen, ask totally unrelated questions, if need be, and show interest if they want to be believable. The more justifiably irate one becomes, the more politically correct and condescending they become. Warren's not the only one who wasn't fooled, though. The published writers as well as some of the veteran attendees sensed the same thing.

wanted someone to hear my story and give me a chance. The one agent I got a hold of on the phone told me I probably didn't stand a chance with no prior publication and having no college degree unless I attended a writers' conference where I could make some contacts. If I'd known it

would've been a total waste of time, I never would've bothered and been alive today. Making matters worse, I was hooked into one of those books doctor's schemes. Yes, it's humiliating to say, but I paid a freelance editor to work on my manuscript who was referred to me by a "potentially" interested agent. Jesus, it still haunts me, all that money I gave her.

I decided to do a very selfish thing. Regardless of knowing that these representatives had no intention of taking on new clients, I was going to pitch my book by the only means I knew how, through Adam. With his looks and his education, I honestly felt I would stand a chance. But I had to get rid of Kate; she would be my ruin, wanting to try and sell that ridiculous manuscript on the perils of child adoption. I mean, come on, haven't the horrors of trying to adopt a kid been played over again and again by *Date Line, 20/20,* and *48 Hours?* It's not as though I was interrupting the most influential novel of the twenty-first century. And it's not as though these two yuppies needed the money either.

It was lucky for me that Adam carried duct tape and rope in a survival kit that he and Kate kept in their Blazer. I don't know how the hell I would explain buying it with Adam's wife in tow. The trick of tying her up was pretty easy, leading her into some kinky sex before the interview to relieve some tension. She was suspicious at first, thinking that I had invaded Adam again, but then that's what she was really hoping for. The good news for her was that I did. The bad news is that death deflates sexual yearnings. Even if I did have any yearnings, with the kind of sense and perception I had of Kate, desire would never entertain my thoughts; plus, being in someone else's body is so uncomfortable that I doubt I could've worked it up anyway. It's like being in an unpleasant smelling gumby suit, only with natural dexterity. I left her tied face down on the bed, spread eagle. Don't worry, she could breathe well through her nose.

The next thing for me to do was get my manuscript in my hands–or well, Adam's hands. Warren still had it in his room, which I could've tried breaking into, but with his room in the center of the balcony on the second floor and exposed to the lobby in the main dorm, the challenge may have got me caught. I had to pretend to be troubled by whatever drove the spirit, or me, to possess my body. I mean Adams body. This possession shit gets confusing.

The conference was having a two-hour lunch before the interviews. Pretty much everyone that didn't volunteer to take the representatives to lunch made a direct path to the main lobby, where they might be able to bolster one another's egos. It was mostly the published authors that took over the responsibility of dining, having the experience and less to lose if they happen to order the wrong appetizer. Some first-year attendees also volunteered in blind faith. In the lobby, I found Warren talking with Oscar and Josslyn. I had to get him away from them.

"Hey Adam…Where's Kate?" I had an urge to tell Oscar that she was tied up at the moment, but that would suggest that she'd be along soon.

"She's back in the room, not feeling well. I don't know if it's her nerves because of the interview or maybe she just had a little too much to drink last night."

"She looked fine at the meeting." Josslyn would

have to put that in.

"Yeah, it came on all of a sudden. That's why I suspect it might be nerves more than anything." I couldn't sense what they were thinking and hated this being one of the other drawbacks of possession.

"Warren, may I speak with you in private?" How's that for subtlety? I had no plan, letting impatience and time get the best of me. Warren gave the other two a quick and barely identifiable puzzled glance.

"Sure," he said, raising his eyelids momentarily. "We'll go up to my room." Okay, so far, so good–just where I wanted to be. Once in Warren's room, he spun a chair around from his desk, said have a seat and sat down at the end of the bed. "What's on your mind, Adam?"

"Ah, since the other night, something's been kind of bothering me. Something you said about reading Jordan's manuscript and that he's lost like the rest of us."

"Yeah, sure, what about it?"

"What did you mean by it?"

"If you read Jordan's story, it tells how the loss of his brother to Vietnam and the fact that his body was never found had been tormenting him almost all of his life. What seems to be pretty obvious is that he loved his brother immensely and never could move on, even as an adult."

"I think, sometimes it's hard when you've had

such an unpleasant experience not to gauge the rest of your life by it."

"Wow man, you sound as though you speak from experience."

"Well, I personally had no comparable experience, but I've read a lot about those sorts of things." It was starting to seem as though the annoying smell in Adam's body was becoming stronger.

"That's a good point, and I guess that makes sense, but from what I gather from reading the story, is that Jordan's brother was the only salvation. Having an abusive father and a drunken mom who was always out with other men made life for him pretty miserable. If it wasn't for the brother stepping in all the time to defend Jordan and take the blame, he probably wouldn't have made it past the seventh grade. And his father getting cancer right after his brother went into the service was a blessing. The old man surely would've beaten poor Jordan to death. He doesn't come right out and say it, but you get the feeling that Jordan holds his brother accountable for all the problems in his life."

"Wait a min. I mean, how can you come to that conclusion?" Warren studied me for a moment. It almost seemed as though he caught a scent of what I was smelling.

"I guess you'd probably have to read the story yourself." This seemed to be my chance.

"I don't suppose you'd let me take it back to my room so I could just glance through it during lunch?"

"Well, you see, I was already supposed to have it back to Joey or Jim so they could send it back to his family. I guess so long as you make sure you have it back to me before dinner, I don't see what the harm would be." Warren got up and pulled the manuscript out of his desk drawer. It was just the way I had sent it. In a black three-ring binder.

"Oh, this is great, Warren. I'm really curious to find out what it's all about. I want to get a little in before the interview sessions, so I think maybe I'll head on back to the room and well. Read a little." I laughed, but I knew it sounded phony. None-the-less, I didn't think it set off any alarms, bells, or whistles.

"Ya probably want to get back and see how Kate is doing?"

"Yeah, right. I'm sure a little rest and she'll be fine."

"Tell her I hope she gets better."

"You bet."

"Oh, and one other thing, Jordan."

"Sure, what's that?"

"Don't forget to return the rental." I was busted. I stood at the door for an instant and dropped my head.

"How'd ya know?"

"When you asked me what I said the other night during the seance. Adam had no recollection of what went on during that time. Your eyes also gave you away. I've seen more death than I want to see, the walking dead of men that knew they were never going to come back home, and those gone but leaving their bodies to pulsate fountains of blood."

"I have to get my manuscript out there, Warren."

"Why? What's it going to solve? You know and I know that your brother is long gone, and you can't resurrect your life, Jordan."

"What the fuck else do I have? In life I was lost and in death I'm completely forgotten. There's no one out there that mourns me."

"There isn't? Who'd you dedicate your book to, Jordan?" I couldn't remember. "Read your title page. What does it say?" I flipped open the binder, and it only took a glimpse. There was my daughter's name, *If ever published I dedicate this to my salvation, Elizabeth.* It all came to me in that simple moment, in that single line.

"You know…it's all there now. I don't know how I could forget her. She meant…No, she means everything to me. She was so excited about me either writing or thinking that I was going to become a writer. I guess I just became too selfish in wanting to tell my story and not a story. You know, she wanted me to write children's stories because she said it would make me happy. It broke my heart at the time she told me because I never thought I was sad around her."

"It sounds like to me, that you were thinking of your daughter. You wanted to make her proud of you. You had a story to tell, sure, we all do, but you were telling it just as much for Elizabeth as you were for yourself."

"I really love her you know. She's the same age right now as I was when my brother died."

"Yeah, I know." I threw the manuscript on the bed.

"If you don't mind, could you please see to it that my daughter gets this."

"You bet I will."

"Before I go to Warren, could you answer me a personal question?"

"Sure, but why don't ya just read my mind?" He smiled.

"I tried but it always seemed blocked by something. You know that most of this is bullshit, so what's the real reason you keep coming to these conferences?"

"That's easy. These people are my friends, for one. You should've been able to read that. Another reason is that it's the one place where who I am and what I do is never questioned. There's a very big chance that I'll never be published, but there's still that one small chance that I will. And even a small chance is something to look forward to. Don't you think?"

"Yeah, I suppose I do. Well, I think I'm going

to go home now."

"Before you go to Jordan, is Kate alright?"

"She's fine. She's, but I'll take care of her before I leave." I left for Adam and Kate's room. When I got inside, I left Adams body. To say the least, he was shocked, but Kate was aware that he wasn't at fault.

I'm watching my daughter grow now, and I know that she really did love me and loves me still. She's independent, takes her mother with a grain of salt, and reads a lot. She has it on her mind that she wants to become a writer. Hopefully that'll change, but there are worse things, I suppose.

She's read my manuscripts over and over again, particularly <u>Open Graves</u>, sneaking it into principal's office and making duplicates on the copier just so she can correct my errors. She gets straight A's in English, you know? She intends to have my stories published someday, but it's enough for me that she reads them, cares, is sensitive, and believes in the impossible.

As far as the conference went, I stayed long enough to see all the writers give their hugs and kisses goodbye until the following year. Everyone was leaving by plane, train, or automobile. It's barely worth mentioning that they'll all probably do it again next year. Unless, of course, they're on a book signing tour. Which could easily be the case for Julie, having been bombarded with calls from her agent, telling her she already has two popular publishing houses that would like to talk over a contract for her next story. But Julie wasn't as excited as the first time when she called everyone she knew after being accepted for publication. This time she didn't even call her folks.

The same could be said for Jeff. After reading his synopsis, Sharon became excited about the idea. Taking it back to her room the same evening, she couldn't put the story down. She swore to Jeff the following day that she knew of several publishers dying to get their hands on children's stories like his. Then added, that for the time being he should keep his occupation as a topless club owner quiet. He assured her that he had every intention of putting the place up for sale as soon as he returned home. Okay, so I wasn't completely on my mark as far as all agents go. But just for the record I didn't explore their subconscious as in depth as I did the other writers. You can say I judged the book by its cover. So, sue me. After all, it was only one author that was recognized out of a possible forty-nine, and time will tell if it still makes it to print or not.

As for the others, I can't say for sure, but there was a strong indication that Oscar was probably going to leave his wife. And Josslyn intended to move out on her own as soon as she got back home so Oscar would have a place to visit.

Denise decided not to do anymore memoirs and returned to the theater. Adam and Kate probably won't be together much longer. That evening, after I tied her up, she asked Adam to do the same, but he adamantly refused, calling her sick.

Noah was inspired to try a different genre and cross over into sci-fi writing. The manuscript he began is about Hitler being an alien from the planet Diovacrell, an inferior planet that accidentally comes across a spacecraft from yet another planet, though much more advanced, that crashes into Diovacrell, killing the crew but not damaging the instrumentation.

May was looking forward to going back to her neighborhood, telling her priest, the ladies at bingo, and her best friend Janette in the building across the street everything that happened at the conference. She was also excited to hear Denise say that she would come to visit her from time to time. Denise appeared to be intent to do so.

Barnell and Katrina struck up a friendship on the last day and promised each other to keep in touch. Katrina found his nervous ticks charming.

Tom expressed that he didn't think he could go without seeing Joan for very long, but she comforted him and told him to deal with it, reassuring him that there's always next year.

Joey couldn't stand it anymore and had sex with Grace, then, while lying in bed, asked her if she was serious about not liking what he wrote, and she said that she liked his as much as he liked hers.

Just as much as Dorothy enjoyed her job as a state trooper and wouldn't give it up for almost anything, well except for a major book deal, Elaine and Lenny had no intention of giving up their jobs at the colleges.

Liz and Beverly left for home, soon after the interviews, but already made plans to attend another conference in New Mexico during the month of June, lasting two weeks.

As for Abigail, her plans were already talked about. And I think she'll do well.

Now will she give up witchcraft entirely? God, I hope not.

Buzz received a call the night after the interviews from an ex-girlfriend who told him he has an eight-year-old son. They dated only twice, but she reminded him that it only takes once. He left the conference soon after the phone call. Her and the boy had been living in Memphis for the last three years, and he wanted to find out if it was really his child or not, thinking some sort of visual comparison might solve the mystery. In some way, he wanted it to be his kid, if just to have an excuse to get out of the relationship he was currently in. Being bisexual, the young man he was living with was beautiful, and at first their friendship seemed extraordinary. Increasingly, though, Buzz found him to be superficial and lately a freeloader. A child would be nice, he thought because he always wanted to be a father.

Jim had two cases going to court the week after his return, so his thoughts were consumed with preparation; he called his intern to research this or that prior to him getting home.

I don't know what to say about Warren. He really seemed to have no plans, and he didn't seem to have any expectations either. He thought about getting the muffler fixed on his truck and maybe getting rid of the snow tires. His brother called and asked if he wanted to go on a fishing trip down in the Keys the following weekend, and of course Warren agreed. But who could turn down a trip like that? Especially when his brother said he'd pay for everything. The only catch was that Warren had to put him in his next story. Warren told him that he'd think about it, and that was good enough.

As for who was making the coffee every morning, that was Warren, up before the others, drinking his coffee, and waiting. He waited for the day to come to life; he waited to observe the living, then hoped to participate, make contact, hear and be heard, touch and be touched, like anyone, I suppose. Sometimes wanting it all in moderation, but most times taking what handouts he could receive. And if you're wondering who wrote this story—a ghostwriter obviously. A fucking ghostwriter who gets to accept all the credit. But that's okay, I couldn't really see myself at a book signing anyway. I just never really had a talent for selling myself.

Finally, for the writers interested in knowing how <u>Coffee With Ghosts</u> was published, assuming it went through the hands of some open minded (or absent-minded, depending on your sympathies) agent and editor that saw past the slander and considered it a work of fiction; or if it went through a vanity press, I couldn't say. From this point on, everything is in the hands of what has been, so far, a very cooperative ghostwriter. Or in this case, a living writer? And if this story is never published, because of censure, quality, or an author who felt violated, I guess there's really nothing more I need to say. Well, for this story anyway. This possession business keeps getting easier and easier the more you do it. Once you get past the smell.

ABOUT THE AUTHOR

Having been a soldier, sailor, carpenter, painter, plumber, surveyor, printing press operator, home health care worker, and maintenance person at a chocolate factory, Craig Rory Draheim's experiences are evident in his story telling, giving him a unique perspective in fiction.

He currently lives in Michigan with his better three quarter, Margaret. They have two sons, Charlie and CR. Draheim has written three other books: Boys of Babylon; Nuts, Bolts, and Monster Worship; and A History Book, Sir Elton John, and the Grasshopper Man.

www.ingramcontent.com/pod-product-compliance
Lightning Source LLC
Chambersburg PA
CBHW032034310726
48972CB00002B/674

9798894790152